# DEATH BY DESSERT

## HEARTS GROVE COZY MYSTERY
### BOOK TEN

### DANIELLE COLLINS

Fairfield Publishing

# CONTENTS

THE MORNING AIR was crisp and tinted with the sea salt aroma one came to expect when near the water. A light breeze blew toward Henrietta Hewitt as she sat on a bench near the pier waiting for the ferry that was carrying Ralph Gershwin across the water from Seattle.

"Oh, *phew*, we made it."

Henrietta turned to see her sister, Clementine Hewitt and Detective Dan Culper, her boyfriend, walking toward where she sat.

"You've got plenty of time." Standing, she embraced her sister when she came near.

"Hey, Henrietta," Dan said, his hand lightly resting on her sister's shoulders. Henrietta nodded at him but turned to study her sister more closely.

Clementine tried to force a smile while patting down her hair, but Henrietta could tell she was nervous. In fact, if she were honest with herself, she was nervous as well. Ralph had been gone for almost a full week on a trip that could bring both she and her sister face to face with her nephew—Clementine's son, Calvin.

Calvin had been missing for years by this point, but it had come to Henrietta's attention when she discovered that her sister was not, in fact, dead. Since that time not only had Henrietta joined her sister in searching for Calvin, but her friend and Private Investigator Ralph and her new employee, Jacob Tait, had been searching as well.

"Jacob's not coming, is he?" Clementine asked. It had quickly become clear to Henrietta that her sister and her new employee hadn't hit things off well. While Jacob was impulsive, he was also young and didn't think his words through like he should. Henrietta had found it necessary to keep them apart for most of the time she and Ralph had spoken with him about what he knew regarding Calvin after his bold claim that he'd met the man.

"No, he's covering the shop while Olivia is home sick."

"Good," she said, though she looked slightly ashamed.

"He was just trying to help," Henrietta said.

"If by help you mean over-exaggerating his information and flat out lying about meeting my son, then yes, he was 'trying to help.'"

It had finally come to light that when Jacob said he'd met Calvin, he'd actually meant online. They'd exchanged a few encrypted emails and Jacob had somewhat befriended Henrietta's nephew. While Clementine had every right to be frustrated at the young man's prideful assertions, Henrietta saw them for what they were. A cry for attention and a sure sign that he needed good, wise supporting friends in his life.

A horn blared and the three turned to see the ferry approaching.

"I hope he has good news."

Henrietta agreed, though she didn't say anything. She had a feeling he would have called if the news was *that* good, but she didn't want to sow any seeds of doubt yet, especially not when they were close to answers.

They began to walk down the boardwalk, the water lapping at the thick logs that jutted down into the water. Seagulls called overhead and a few others milled about the area. While Henrietta called Heart's Grove home, she often made the forty-five minute trip to Port Angeles, Washington in order to shop or take the ferry to Seattle or any number of things the larger city afforded.

Now though, her focus was on the incoming boat. A few passengers stood on the upper deck, taking in the last of the scenery before they docked, though Henrietta didn't see Ralph among them.

After a few more minutes of silence between the

three, the ship docked and a gangplank extended to the dock. The first passengers began to filter out and soon Henrietta spotted Ralph. He wore a puffy jacket with jeans and his typical baseball cap. One hand was in his pocket while the other pulled a small, black rolling suitcase. He always seemed to travel light and Henrietta wasn't quite sure how he did it.

He nodded, acknowledging them, and made a beeline toward their little group.

"There he is," Clementine said, stating the obvious. "I hope it's good news."

"It'll be okay, honey," Dan said.

Henrietta sent him a sidelong glance out of curiosity. A few months prior Dan had shown interest in her, but she had not returned the feelings. While she wasn't *attached* to anyone, she did find that Ralph's company was the only kind of the male persuasion she wanted to keep.

Now, seeing him ruddy cheeked and not quite smiling, she thought again of how handsome he was but also how his countenance, usually congenial, didn't lend itself to good news.

Bracing herself, Henrietta smiled warmly at him and asked, "How was the trip?"

An innocent question that could be taken any way, but everyone there knew what she meant. It wasn't a pleasure trip.

"I've got good news," he said, looking at Clementine, "and bad." He finished by turning to

Henrietta, perhaps because he knew she could handle the bad along with the good.

"B-bad news?" Clementine said.

"And good," Henrietta pointed out, resting her hand on her sister's arm. "Let's go sit and you can tell us how it went."

Ralph nodded and they walked over to a small area where several benches sat, some facing one another. Henrietta and Ralph took one while Clementine and Dan took the other.

"Please, tell us what happened," Clementine said.

"He will," Dan assured her, resting his hand atop her clenched ones.

Henrietta could see the strength he lent her sister and felt her tense shoulders relax some. While she hadn't anticipated Dan and her sister's relationship, she found that it had a true quality to it she appreciated. Dan was a good guy and a very good detective and, while he worked in Port Angeles, he made frequent trips to Heart's Grove to visit her sister. He was a good guy and Henrietta was determined to tell him that someday...though right now was not that time.

"I'll start with the bad." Ralph looked at them then drilled his stare into Clementine. "I couldn't find your son at the location Jacob gave me."

She inhaled sharply and leaned back though she didn't say anything, likely sensing Ralph wasn't done yet.

"I took the full week because I ended up chasing

down some leads in hopes that he'd just moved or was still in the area but it does look like he is no longer in Virginia. If it means anything, I will say that I think he *was* there though, so that's something."

"But, what does that mean?" Clementine asked.

"It's a good thing that Ralph apparently found evidence that your son was in Virginia," Dan explained. "It means at least some of our information was correct."

"Yes, but also some of it was wrong. The address that was included in the letter you got was certainly fake," Ralph explained, referring to the letter that Clementine had gotten from Calvin saying he was in trouble and needed help. He had asked her to wire money and, while it had taken everything in her arsenal to convince her sister *not* to send the money, she had only pacified her by coming up with the idea to hire Ralph and send him to Virginia.

"It was fake?" Clementine said.

"Very, but I did find a few helpful things through those connections."

"Like?" Dan asked.

"Like an email address that is supposedly connected to Calvin as well as a phone number."

"A number?" Clementine's eyes went wide.

"Yes. Though I didn't call it––I thought that the first call should come from you."

She nodded.

Henrietta caught the look that Dan gave Ralph and

surmised that they were both thinking what she had been; if there was a phone number, there was the possibility to trace it. It was likely that they would be bringing Scott Gershwin, Ralph's son, in on this soon.

"Is that the g-good news?" Clementine sniffled.

"It is, and I realize that doesn't seem like much, but I do think it's a strong lead to go with. I will compile the evidence I came up with and start working the next angle of this case."

Clementine looked like she wanted to ask what that was but instead she leaned into Dan. "Can you take me home?"

He looked surprised but Henrietta nodded. "That's probably wise. We'll keep you posted on what we come up with, Clem, but remember this—we're looking for him and we have good leads. It's more than we had a week ago."

"That's true," she agreed. "It's just…hard. Is he in trouble?"

Three sets of eyes turned to Ralph and he tossed up his hands. "It's hard to say for certain."

Henrietta read between the lines of that statement and in that moment realized he must have found more than he'd let on. And, for some reason, he was keeping that part to himself. Why he would do that she wasn't certain, but she felt he must have a good reason to do so.

"Let's get back to Heart's Grove," Henrietta said,

7

looking over at Ralph. "I can take you back, Clementine."

"It's all right," Dan said with a grin. "I'll take her. We're going to go see a movie tonight—take our minds off of this for just a few hours—so I'll be needing to head that way anyway. Plus, don't you have that sardine can of a car?"

Henrietta surprised him by laughing. "My Mini Cooper? I find that it's just the right size for me."

"You and maybe one other person," Dan countered.

She shrugged, "Ralph could fit in the back seat."

"I'll do no such thing," he said, adjusting the handle of his suitcase. "Let's go, Henri."

And with that, they set off for her car.

---

"ALL RIGHT, Mr. Gershwin, spill the beans." Henrietta put the car in drive and pulled out onto the main road that would lead them toward Heart's Grove along the coast.

"Your sister's...delicate," he said after a moment of thought. "I did share the pertinent details, but there were a few other things I thought better of telling her."

"I understand," Henrietta said. "I'm not chastising you, but I do expect to be filled in."

She caught his grin out of the corner of her eye. "I know you do."

"Well?" She stopped at a red light and looked over at him expectantly.

"I'm trying to think of the best way to start."

"The beginning," she said simply and accelerated when the light turned green.

"Okay, first things first, Calvin was there—and maybe as close as two or three days before I arrived."

"You think he caught wind of you coming and left?"

"I think that's exactly what happened."

"But why?" Henrietta shot him another quick look, assessing his facial features and trying to read what he wasn't saying.

"I honestly don't know, Henri."

She wrinkled her nose at the nickname Ralph insisted on calling her. "Hypothesize then. It's me—Henrietta—I'm here to listen."

"Right, right," he rubbed at his jaw, the sound of the stubble there making a scratching noise. "I think he was, or is, into something deep. I think that he might actually be in trouble, but I don't think he sent that letter to Clementine."

"I agree," she added as a side note.

"But I also think that he may be conflicted about coming 'home' if you will."

"How so?"

"If a kid knows his mom, and now his aunt, are looking for him, and he's done any kind of research on you, he's got to know your, uh, reputation."

"You say that like selling antiques is akin to drug dealing," she said, her tone snarky.

"Hardly. I'm talking about the...money."

This time when her eyes left the road they were burning and turned on Ralph like a sniper's sight. "What?"

"I'm not saying it's public knowledge, but if Calvin is mixed up with anyone worth their salt, they are going to find out that there is some money to be had."

Henrietta sighed. She hadn't accounted for that, in fact, she never really paid much thought to the wealth she'd accumulated first as an accountant for a large firm and then as an antiques dealer.

"But what if that's off the table."

"How so?"

"Let's say it isn't a known variable. What else could be going on?"

"Okay, yeah." Ralph sighed and she could almost hear his thinking. "I'd say that maybe you've got a kid up to his eyeballs in something bad—I don't know how bad, but enough that maybe he promised someone they could get a decent payoff if they acted like him. You know, bought himself some time to get away."

Henrietta nodded. "That could work. So, maybe he got wind of your arrival and then used a ploy to get away. But no, that doesn't work."

"Yeah," Ralph grunted. "I see my mistake. How would he have known to send the letter before I even decided to come visit him?"

"What if your arrival wasn't the catalyst for him leaving? What if it was something else?" Henrietta mused.

"That would make sense, but it won't get us closer to knowing what it was. I tell you what, this kid was a ghost." Ralph readjusted in his seat, his long legs cramped in the small car.

"What do you mean?"

"He was clean in leaving. Took it all, covered his tracks—mostly—and told no one he was leaving."

"What was he doing in Virginia?"

"Working construction so I hear, though interior stuff during the winter. Corporate, I think. His coworkers said he was a nice guy, kept to himself, didn't seem to have a girlfriend. Said he'd gone out with them maybe twice but most of the time declined their offers. I checked his apartment but it was empty, like *wiped down* empty."

"Interesting."

"Yeah, the only other thing I found out was that he paid for everything in cash. Rent, phone bill, at the restaurant with his coworkers. People said they saw him with lots of cash often."

"Oh no," Henrietta said. "Drugs?"

"I thought of that too," Ralph admitted. "But everyone seemed to think he was a straight arrow. Said he only ordered soda when he went out with them."

"Interesting."

"Will you stop saying that?" Ralph said. "What else is going on in that mind of yours?"

"I'm not sure," she said, taking a steep curve at a fast pace but executing it perfectly.

"Why don't I believe you?"

"I don't know enough. Though I do think we need to talk to Jacob after this visit you've had. While he may not have actually *met* my nephew, he did 'meet up' with him online several times. I'm curious to see if he can still reach out to him and what else he can tell us."

"I agree. That kid's a wily one. His info was good, but slightly outdated."

"And a large part of me wonders how that is possible."

"*Mhmph.*"

The center of Heart's Gove came into view and Henrietta slowed down. She made the circle around the center of the town monument and then headed toward her antique shop, H.H. Antiques, where Ralph had parked his truck.

"He's working today," Henrietta said, "but I don't think now is the right time. We need to go over what you found, I'm assuming you took photos and have documents, etc. Then, when we have a better idea and can ask better questions, we'll bring Jacob in."

"You're some firecracker," Ralph said with a chuckle, "But I couldn't have said it better."

"Oh," she said, nearing the shop, "I almost forgot.

Sassy is having a tasting tonight; would you like to go with me?"

"Uh—a what?"

"A tasting. Like a wine or coffee tasting but with chocolate."

"I've never heard of that."

"I'm sure others have done it," Henrietta said, pulling up beside Ralph's truck, "but I wanted to go to support her—and tasting chocolate sounds delightful, does it not?"

Ralph tossed up his hands. "I can't say no to chocolate and I certainly can't say no to you. What time?"

"Seven," she said with a smile and a wink. "See you there."

## 2

THE RICH SCENT of chocolate greeted Henrietta and Ralph as they walked into Sassy's Sweets located a few blocks down the street from H.H. Antiques. Henrietta paused to take in a deep breath and then smiled over at Ralph.

"Aren't you glad you agreed to come?"

"Where's the chocolate?" he said in reply.

She laughed and pulled him toward the back room of the shop that Sassy reserved for special parties. The smells of sugar and cocoa beans mingled with the scent of coffee and Henrietta smiled to see her friend Gina Russo prepping a coffee bar.

"Gina, I didn't know you were going to be here tonight," she said, giving her friend a quick side hug.

"What goes better with chocolate than coffee?" Gina said.

"Cake," Ralph supplied. Both women ignored him.

"That's a great idea. Are you doing hot chocolate too?"

Gina held a finger to her lips. "I'm sworn to secrecy about what is going on here tonight."

"All right then," Henrietta said, smiling and holding up her hands in surrender. "You do what you do best, coffee."

"You know it."

"Henrietta, Ralph, I'm so glad you could make it."

They turned to see Sassy. She wore a broad, bright smile that matched her white chef's coat that hugged her curvy frame. Standing a few inches shorter than Henrietta's short frame the woman was small but mighty.

"Wouldn't have missed it for the world," Henrietta said.

"I'm here for the chocolate," Ralph deadpanned.

Sassy laughed, the sound ringing out through the empty space. "I just hope others come for the chocolate too."

Henrietta noticed the woman was wringing her hands together. "You've gotten RSVPs, haven't you?"

"Yes," she nodded, "but you never know. Things come up. People can't make it. Things like that."

"Hope they paid in advance," Ralph muttered.

Henrietta shot him a look before turning back to Sassy. "It's going to be fine, you'll see."

Just then the front doorbell rang, and Henrietta winked at her friend who hurried to the front.

"Ralph," Henrietta chided, seeing that he'd already made himself a cup of coffee.

"What?" he shrugged. "They wouldn't have put it out if it wasn't for us."

"Yes, but what if Sassy wanted to wait on that."

"I'm on East Coast time, remember?"

Henrietta grimaced. "I had forgotten that. You could have declined the invitation," she said, softening toward her friend.

"I wanted to come," he said, then his eyes met hers, "it's good to see you Henrietta. I…wanted to spend time with you."

She blushed. Though they'd been on a few dates, their relationship, or whatever they were calling this, was still very new to her. Over the last few months Henrietta had begun to realize that she had issues with commitment. While she valued Ralph's friendship and trusted him as a friend, she wasn't sure what her heart would allow beyond that.

"Hey," he said, gaining her attention again, "it's okay."

Sighing, she turned her attention toward the door. Now was not the time to contemplate her relationship with Ralph Gershwin, no matter how *known* he made her feel. He could tell that she resisted his gentle advancements and yet he kept trying. Perhaps one day she'd welcome them rather than push them away.

A couple entered the room, the woman tall and thin, her husband slightly shorter and a little rounder than her. She had her hand slung through his arm despite the slightly awkward angle and the two seemed to be very much in love.

"Angela, Tim, this is Henrietta and Ralph. They were my first guests tonight," Sassy said by way of introduction.

"Nice to meet you," Tim said, shaking their hands.

"Likewise," Ralph said.

"Newlyweds?" Henrietta asked.

"How'd you guess?" Angela said through a giggle.

"You've got that newly-wed glow about you."

More smiling, and if Henrietta wasn't mistaken, Tim was actually blushing. The doorbell rang again and Sassy slipped away.

"How'd you hear about the tasting?" Henrietta asked.

"We were looking for things to do around town—there's not much," Angela admitted.

"I like chocolate," Tim said with a shrug.

"It's a good enough reason," Henrietta admitted with a laugh just as Sassy came back through the door with three women trailing after her. Henrietta recognized one.

"Ethel, good to see you," she said, approaching the older woman and leaving Ralph to talk to the newlyweds.

"Oh Henrietta, so nice to see you. You haven't been to book club in a month of Sundays," she admonished.

"I haven't," Henrietta admitted. "I've been busy plus

my sister moved to town so I've been spending time with her." She mentally added that she'd also been solving crimes and searching for her nephew. Busy was an understatement.

"How nice. Bring her to book club," the woman said with a grin. "Oh, is that coffee?" She made a beeline for the coffee pot and Henrietta turned to the other ladies with Sassy.

"Hello, my name is Henrietta," she said, approaching the small group.

"Hi, I'm Barbara," the older one said.

"I'm Leslie, her sister," the other woman said with a grin.

Henrietta could see the family resemblance with the dark hair and same blue eyes.

"Nice to meet you," Henrietta said but her next question was cut off by the look on Sassy's face.

"Sassy—" Henrietta began but she followed her friend's gaze to a man who stood in the doorway. In fact, she noticed that everyone in the room was staring at him.

He was tall with thinning hair and a gaunt expression. He looked out of place in the white space with his dark shirt and black jeans. It was his eyes that caused Henrietta to take a closer look though. It looked like a spark of recognition she saw on her friend's face, but it didn't appear to create happiness in her friend.

"Uh, Mark," Sassy said, stepping toward him. "I didn't expect to see you here."

Her friend was uneasy, that much was easy enough to deduce, but the reason as to why would be much harder, especially with the space quickly filling with people. As Henrietta looked around, she noticed that nearly everyone was shooting the man odd looks. It was clear that he didn't belong, he wasn't dressed for an evening of chocolate tasting, but that didn't seem to bother him.

Ralph came up to Henrietta and whispered, "Who's that?"

"I don't know."

Just then Ethel came back into the circle. "Good coffee, you ladies should grab some. Bet you anything it's from Gina's shop."

Henrietta's gaze was still on the quiet exchange the man was having with Sassy. He glanced up, looking at the group, and his expression seemed to darken. Then, abruptly, her friend turned toward the small group, bright patches of pink on her cheeks.

"Um, if you'll all excuse me. I'll go ready the first course. Please, take your seats and we'll start the tasting soon."

Sassy disappeared into the kitchen and the group found their spots, marked by small cards, around the table. But, before she could sit down, Henrietta made up her mind to go see if her friend was all right.

"I'll be right back."

"Don't interfere with lovers' quarrels," Ralph advised. "It never goes well."

While Henrietta hadn't exactly pegged the man Sassy had called Mark as a lover, she wasn't too certain part of what Ralph said was true.

"I'll be right back," she repeated.

In the back room she found Sassy in a corner with her back to the door.

"Sassy?" Henrietta asked gently.

The woman jumped as if she'd been electrocuted and spun around, blocking what was behind her. "Henrietta, is something wrong?" she said, nervously smoothing a piece of hair behind her ear.

"I," Henrietta proceeded carefully, "I was just seeing if you're all right?"

"I—oh I'm fine," she said, sniffing and trying to brighten her smile. "Just a little surprised is all."

"About the man—Mark?"

Sassy's eyes widened but her look of surprise quickly turned to one of chagrin. "You don't miss anything, do you Henrietta?"

"Not often," she said without pretense. "What is it? Who is he to you?"

"Oh goodness," she said, shaking her head. "It's a foolish, long story. Suffice it to say we once went on a few dates and things didn't work out. I just wasn't expecting him to be here tonight."

"Then I'm guessing he didn't pay beforehand?"

"No. But that's all right. If he's going to pay the cover, I'm okay with it." She forced a laugh. "Now go back in there and *relax*. No sleuthing needed here."

Henrietta still felt like there was something her friend wasn't saying, but she didn't feel that it was the time to press the issue so she capitulated and returned to the tasting room and a seat next to Ralph who wore a look that said 'I told you so'.

The next twenty minutes were filled with chocolates and cooling sorbet to cleanse the palate between each tasting. They tried dark, milk, white, and flavored chocolates. For Henrietta, the coffee cream, a combined effort between Gina and Sassy, was her favorite, though Ralph was partial to the dark chocolate Moroccan mint truffle Sassy had created.

Finally, the last round appeared. Sassy had been talking it up the whole night and Henrietta could tell everyone was excited to discover Sassy's newest creation that would be added to her menu.

Their portion came out on mini platters with covers and, on the count of three, they all unmasked the chocolate.

Henrietta frowned and met Sassy's gaze with a questioning one of her own. They all looked exactly like the truffles they'd been trying the whole night except for a fine, reddish powder on the top. Sassy grinned to answer their curious looks.

"I'm keeping this one a surprise until after you taste it. I've only given you a slight hint. I'll likely make it more elaborate when I create the real thing for the shop, but I don't want any preconceived notions. *Bon appetit!*"

As a group, each picked up the truffle and tasted it. Immediately, Henrietta felt a heat on the back of her tongue. It wasn't wholly unpleasant but decidedly different. Ralph made a surprised, grunting sound and seemed to be enjoying the *hot* chocolate.

But then the sound of gagging across the table drew everyone's attention. Mark was leaning forward, a hand at his throat coughing. Soon he had pushed his chair back and was on his feet as if trying to draw in more air.

"Sir?" Henrietta said, unsure if he was choking or perhaps having some sort of allergic reaction. Her gaze darted to Sassy who looked frozen in horror. "Ralph, call 9-1-1," Henrietta demanded.

He did and then handed his phone to Ethel next to him as he rushed to Mark's side. Soon, Mark slid to his knees, his breathing ragged and thin. The next instant he was on the ground, gasping for air.

As Ralph attempted to help him, Henrietta took the phone from Ethel and explained what was happening, but by the time the paramedics got there it was too late.

Mark was dead.

## 3

HENRIETTA RUBBED slow circles on Sassy's back as Detective Abraham Paige moved toward them. The rest of the tasting members had already been questioned and were about to be released but Sassy still hadn't had a chance to talk to Abe yet.

Waiting around had been an easy decision and Ralph had occupied himself by drinking coffee and eating more chocolates than anyone should have been allowed to. Henrietta, however, had sat with Sassy reassuring her that it certainly looked like Mark had succumbed to an allergic reaction. Something that Sassy would have had no way of knowing.

"Miss Roberts," Abe said, approaching. "Hello, Henrietta."

"Good evening, Detective Paige," she said with a kind smile. The formality was really only for Sassy, but she saw his eyes narrow in question.

"May I ask you both a few questions?"

"Of course," Henrietta said. Sassy merely nodded.

"Did you have a way of knowing allergies before this tasting happened?" he asked.

The question sounded routine, but it also niggled at the back of Henrietta's mind. Was that why he was here? A homicide detective at an apparent accident case? Or had he drawn some short straw, if that were even possible.

"I—I had something in the online sign up form. It asked for allergies just in case but...Mark, uh Mr. Wharton, didn't fill that out. He just showed up and I had no idea he was allergic."

"I see," Abe scribbled in his small notebook. "And the last chocolate, who else knew you'd be serving that tonight?"

Sassy blinked several times. "I—what do you mean?"

"Did you tell anyone what your menu was? Did your tasting attendees know the line-up?"

"No. I mean, I didn't tell anyone specifically about the last truffle being a new one to me. I...it was a surprise."

"So, no one else knew there would be chili peppers in it?"

"No," she said, shaking her head. "Why? Was that what...was he allergic?"

"It appears to be that way, but we're not sure of anything just yet."

Sassy began to cry, her hands shaking as she wiped at her tears. "This was not how tonight was supposed to go."

"Did you know Mr. Wharton before tonight, Miss Roberts?"

Sassy stilled. "I did," she admitted.

"How?" he pressed, but to Henrietta it seemed as if he might already know how and wanted to confirm that with Sassy herself.

"We dated a few times. That was all. It didn't end super well, but nothing bad." She turned pale. "I mean, I didn't put chilies in his chocolate on purpose if that's what you think."

"Just routine questions," he assured her, but Henrietta felt there might be more to them than he'd let on.

"And Henrietta," he turned his attention to her. "You were here for the tasting?"

She gave him a look that said something along the lines of, *That's the best question you have for me?* But rather than voice that she nodded. "Yes. I brought Ralph. We like chocolate," she said with a half-smile.

"Yes, well, did you know the vic-uh, Mr. Wharton?"

His mistake hadn't gotten past her, though she doubted Sassy had caught it. So, there was something here that made Abe think it was a homicide. What exactly had the coroner found?

"No," she finally answered. "Tonight was the first time I'd met him."

"All right," Abe said. "And can you relay what happened tonight? Exactly."

She explained everything in detail, and he took notes though she doubted it was any different from what the rest had told him or his men. Still, she wanted to be as accurate as possible and offered details that others may not have given. Details that could end up being helpful, maybe.

"Thank you," he said when she was done. "And Miss Roberts?"

"Yes?" Sassy said, as if waking from a dream—or perhaps a nightmare in this case.

"We're going to need to ask you not to open tomorrow. My team needs to look into this and it could take a few days. Will you make a sign or something for the front? And then, please don't leave town."

His words, though spoken harmlessly and in an effort to sound normal, had a dramatic effect on Sassy.

"Leave town? What are you saying, Detective Paige? Am I a—a suspect or something?"

"We need everyone involved to remain in close proximity in case a question arises that might help us get to the bottom of this."

"The bottom of—" Sassy's voice rose. "This was an *accident*. He clearly reacted badly to whatever was in the chocolate. I mean, it wasn't done on purpose. Why would you treat me like a suspect for that? Is something else going on that I should be made aware of or—"

"Miss Roberts," he began.

"Please, just give me a straight answer."

"Sassy," Henrietta said in a calming tone. "Don't take offense to what he's saying. It's routine." She hated that word but couldn't think of a better way to put it.

Her words seemed to have a calming effect on her friend who took in a deep breath. "You're right, I'm sorry Detective Paige. Forgive me. It's been an... emotional night." He nodded his assent and she rose. "I'll go make that sign now."

He watched her go but then Henrietta stood up, moving closer. "What is this all about, Abe?"

While their initial interactions hadn't been on the best of terms, Henrietta had slowly come to see Abe as a smart and intuitive detective. He was young, shaking things up in the small community, but he kept the people's safety and the good of the community in the forefront of his mind which made it easier to respect and trust him. He'd also visibly softened toward Henrietta and now seemed to be doing so again.

"I can't say for certain," he began.

"But you've got an idea. A guess, perhaps?"

He made a face. No detective liked to share their hunches.

"You think he was targeted," Henrietta filled in the silence between them.

He looked impressed. "I don't know that I would

have put it quite like that but…it seems odd that one of the special courses—in chocolate mind you—would have chili peppers in it. Something our victim was deathly allergic to."

"And that's why you're here. He's a victim."

"The chief put me on this case because of who the victim is."

"And who is that?" she pressed.

"A man who is running for city council."

"I…" then it struck Henrietta where she'd seen the name before. "How did I miss that? His name is all over signs in people's yards."

"You shock me, Henrietta," Abe said with a grin. "You're supposed to catch onto these things much more quickly than that." His gentle chastisement was well placed though she was loath to admit it. Then again, she had been dealing with a lot, including the case of her missing nephew.

"Maybe I'm losing my touch," she joked.

"I doubt it. We all have our off days. Anyway, I've got to get back to the station. Don't say anything, got it?"

"Naturally," she agreed.

"And Henrietta?"

"Yes?" she said, meeting his gaze.

"Don't let Ralph eat any more of our evidence." With that he was gone.

Henrietta rolled her eyes and went to intercept Ralph on his way to get a coffee refill.

"Isn't it close to your bedtime?"

"What, this stuff? It won't affect me."

"I doubt that, but it is time to go."

He nodded and after saying goodbye to Sassy and making sure she could get home safely, they left to walk back to the shop. It was chilling out, much colder than when they had set out before, and Henrietta almost regretted not bringing a heavier scarf.

"What do you make of all that?" Ralph said, his breath fogging out before him.

"I'm not sure."

"What did the kid say?"

Henrietta laughed. "You've got to stop referring to every person under forty as a 'kid' Ralph."

"I can't help it if they decided to fill the Lead Detective role with a baby." He made a face. While he and Abe hadn't gotten along at all at first, they'd come around to a tenuous relationship of mutual trust.

"He seems to think that this wasn't accidental."

"Yup."

"You say that like you were already thinking that."

"I *am* a private detective. In case you'd forgotten."

"I had not," she said, not giving him the satisfaction of even a sideways glance.

"I happened to take a closer look at the fella's chocolate."

"Oh?"

"Before the police swarmed the place, of course."

"And what did you see?"

29

"Lots, and I mean *lots*, of chili flakes."

"Flakes?"

He nodded. "I mean, that thing could have knocked over a rhino." She made a face and he shrugged. "You know what I mean."

"I'm afraid I do," she said, though more to herself.

"This doesn't look good for Sassy."

"But she had no idea he was coming to the tasting. He didn't fill out an online form and just showed up. Likely she would have taken the spicy chocolate off the menu had she known."

"Then the question becomes who did know he was coming and how did they swap out the chocolate for a tainted one."

Henrietta sighed. "This is getting complicated."

"More than it was?" Ralph asked as they neared the shop.

"Yes. Sassy claimed that no one knew about her spicy chocolate as the last tasting. If that's true, no one could have planned that but her."

"*Eeesh.*"

"Indeed," Henrietta agreed with Ralph's sentiment.

They arrived at the shop and Ralph bid her goodnight but not before reassuring her that they would keep looking into Calvin's whereabouts in the next few days. She knew it was what they needed to do, it's what she wanted to do as well, but the death tonight made Henrietta more worried about her friend and what the police might uncover and whether or not it would be true evidence or something planted.

If there was one thing she knew, it was that Sassy Roberts was no murderer and if it looked like it had been done on purpose, someone was behind it and that meant someone meant to frame her friend. Something Henrietta would not let happen.

## 4

WHEN OLIVIA SHOWED up for work the next morning she looked tired and as if she still might be fighting off whatever had caused her illness the day before. But she insisted on working, no matter how many times Henrietta told her she could go home and she'd call in Jacob to work in her place.

"If I'm not careful, Jacob's going to take over my job," she said with a smirk.

"Never," Henrietta countered. "He doesn't have the degree you do nor does he have quite the same charm with customers."

Olivia grinned and began to catalogue a new shipment they had received the day before while Henrietta read the local newspaper. The death from the night before was, unsurprisingly, front page news.

"A shame," Henrietta muttered to herself.

Olivia came up behind her and let out a breath.

"That is so sad. Poor Sassy—to have an accident like that on your *first* tasting? I hope she can recover from that."

While Henrietta didn't say it out loud, she hoped the same thing.

"Was the rest of it good though?" Olivia asked with a grimace.

"She was doing such a wonderful job. Each chocolate had a background and she explained the inspiration for each. It was just lovely all around, until the last course."

"And to think he was deathly allergic to chilies and that was her last course. What are the odds?" Olivia said it in an offhanded way that showed she wasn't thinking of the ramifications of her statement, but Henrietta was.

What exactly *were* the odds of that? High, that was for sure. And with that in mind, she put in a call to Olivia's husband and Ralph's son, Scott.

"Hey Henrietta," he said upon answering the phone on the second ring.

She'd moved to the front room so as not to alert Olivia to her suspicions just yet. "I was wondering if you could do something for me."

"Uh oh," he said in a joking manner. "I know whenever you say that I'm likely about to break a law of some sort."

"Now don't say that," she teased. "I just want to get a little background information on Mark Wharton."

"The guy who died last night at the tasting?"

"Yes. That's the one. I believe he's also running for city council?"

"You're in luck," he said and she heard his keys typing in the background. "Dad asked me to do the same thing so I've got a head start though it's looking a little more involved than just a simple background check."

"Why is that?"

"On the surface he looks legit. Normal life, bank account, business stuff, all of that, but when I hacked— er, looked into his computer and other bank records, I found some anomalies."

"As in?"

"Offshore money. Possibly some shady business dealings hidden under a shell corporation. Stuff like that. I don't have a full perspective on it yet though so you'll have to wait a little longer."

Henrietta knew that patience was key in solving mysteries and it seemed this one would be no different. "Sounds good. Please call me when you can with what you know."

"You got it."

She ended the call and turned to look out the window just in time to see her sister rushing up the steps toward the front door.

"Good morning, Clem," she said as her sister rushed inside, pulling her scarf down from her neck.

"Oh, Henrietta," she said, the exasperation and

dramatic nature of the way she said it putting Henrietta immediately on edge.

"What is it?"

"I just," she shook her head, tossing her hands up in the air, "I just know you're going to get sucked into another case and totally forget about Calvin."

This shocked Henrietta and she shifted from one foot to the other before answering her sister. "What makes you think that?"

"I saw the paper. You'd mentioned to me yesterday you were going to that tasting and I know you're friends with the shop owner. Something's going to happen and you'll be called in and—I just can't live without knowing where Calvin is."

"Calm down, Clem." Henrietta rested a hand on her sister's shoulder.

"Don't tell me to calm down. This is my son we're talking about."

In that moment it all came back to Henrietta. The way her sister had acted when they were little. If she didn't get her way she'd become overly dramatic, just like this. It wasn't necessarily a fault because, of course, she cared deeply about her son, but she also wasn't seeing things in perspective.

"Ralph is working on follow up from his trip right now, he texted me that this morning. I know that Jacob has agreed to help us with the new email address and tracking that as well. We need to be patient because things like this don't work themselves out overnight."

Clementine sniffed. "I know, I just feel so helpless."

And there was the root of it all. Her sister didn't know what she could do so she took it out on Henrietta. It wasn't that Henrietta agreed with that, but at least she could understand where Clementine was coming from.

"I understand, but I need you to trust us. Trust that we'll let you know what happens and that we'll keep you in the loop."

"But will you?" she pressed.

Another good question. Ralph hadn't told her everything, but it was precisely for this reason. Dramatic responses wouldn't get them anywhere.

"Yes, when the information is helpful."

Her sister's eyes narrowed. "What does that mean."

"If something looks one way but isn't proven, why share that theory until we're certain. You must understand that with where you work. Doctor Swinson doesn't give a guess about what might be wrong with his patients, he waits until the tests are in. Think of what we're doing like that."

Clementine took a deep breath and let it out. "That does make sense." Henrietta could tell her sister was calming down. "I'm sorry. I just spent so much of last night imagining the worst scenarios about Calvin and why he hadn't contacted me. I mean, he had every means to do so and still has stayed away."

"He must have a good reason," Henrietta added.

"I suppose so. But...I'm his mom. Regardless of

what happened when he was a kid, I hope he would know I love him."

Henrietta recalled some of what her sister had shared about Calvin's childhood being somewhat chaotic, but she'd tried to make amends which had to count for something.

"We'll find him, and you can ask him those questions yourself."

Clementine offered a watery smile and Henrietta pulled her in for a hug. "Are you on a lunch break?" she asked when they pulled apart.

"Yeah, I told them I needed to make an errand. They probably think I'm scatterbrained today but I just couldn't focus. I needed to talk to you."

"Well please don't worry. I think that last night's incident was an accident and—" Her cell phone rang and she looked down at the caller ID to see it was a call from the police station.

"What's wrong?" Clementine said.

"Nothing," Henrietta said with a smile. "But I need to take this. Don't worry, all right?'

"I'll try," Clementine said before she turned to leave.

Henrietta turned her back as she answered, "Hello?"

"Henrietta?"

"Sassy?"

"Oh, my goodness, Henrietta. They took me in for questioning. I'm at the police station. I—I think they think I killed Mark."

5

HENRIETTA WALKED the familiar sidewalk toward the police station. Not one to beat around the bush, Henrietta had told Sassy she'd be right down and had all but hung up on the woman. Clearly something was going on and she wanted to get to the bottom of it.

At the front desk she was assigned a visitor's pass and Detective Paige met her at the front door.

"I figured she might call you," he said, holding the door open for her.

"Should she have called a lawyer first?" Henrietta asked, her bluntness no surprise to Abe.

"I'm not one to advise on that but if she has nothing to hide what can be gained from lawyering up?"

"You know as well as I do that sometimes even those who tell the truth get punished for it."

He gave her a conciliatory look and directed her

toward his desk first. He motioned for her to have a seat and after clearing with her that she didn't want any coffee or water, he perched on the edge of his desk.

"You might want to ask your friend about Mark. The full story, perhaps?"

"Will you be listening in?"

"Undecided," he said, though she had a feeling he wasn't above snooping. Then again, if this was not a murder investigation, he'd have every right to find out everything he could.

"Has she told you the truth?"

"No, but I can see what it looks like."

It was on the tip of Henrietta's tongue to ask what he meant but he continued.

"Like I said, better to get the truth from your friend, but it doesn't look good."

In that moment Henrietta made a decision. "If she's all right with it, why don't you come in and we can all talk."

"Uh, all right."

"But let me talk with her first?"

"Of course."

He led Henrietta to an interrogation room and allowed her to enter. She knew there was a two-way mirror on one side but nothing she said would be too personal or would, hopefully, incriminate her friend. At least she didn't think it would.

"Oh, thank goodness you're here, Henrietta." Sassy

stood and accepted Henrietta's embrace. "I don't know what is going on. It's like my life has entered the *Twilight Zone* or something."

"Sassy," she said, resting her hand on her friend's arm. "I think you should talk to Detective Paige, with me here, and get the truth in the open."

"The truth?" she looked shocked but Henrietta rushed to explain.

"I'm sorry, I don't mean that you're hiding something but I think there are some unanswered questions."

Her friend's expression fell. "I think I know what you mean. Yes, that detective can come in. I'll answer his questions. But I want you to stay."

"Absolutely."

Henrietta stepped out and motioned Abe in. He sat on the other side of Henrietta facing Sassy and deferred to what Henrietta would say.

"Sassy, I know that all of this is…shocking. I don't know the full extent either, but from the sound of it, there is more about Mark than what you're letting on."

Sassy's shoulders slumped and she nodded. "I'm sorry I didn't tell you last night, Detective Paige, but yes, there is more to the story."

"Why don't you go ahead and tell me now?" he offered.

She nodded and began. "I met Mark several years ago. He was actually my realtor who helped me purchase the shop."

Henrietta frowned. She remembered the time when Sassy was getting ready to open her shop and, if her memory served her, the process hadn't been smooth.

"But, before any of that," Sassy said, interrupting Henrietta's thoughts, "we had gone on a few dates. He was kind, funny, and took me to nice places. I was falling fast when he told me about the storefront opening."

"Sounds like things were going well," Abe said.

"They were, or so I thought. I'll admit that I was more distracted by this potential relationship with Mark than I was about the details. Never again," she shook her head.

"What do you mean?" Henrietta asked.

"I can't prove that this was his motive, but it appeared that Mark had taken me on dates and distracted me with the thought of a relationship so that, when the time came for the deal on the storefront to go through, I didn't look into it all that much. I mean, why should I? It's why I had a realtor and one that was already dating me would surely have my best interests in mind, right?"

"And he didn't," Abe guessed.

"I should have gone with my gut and rented first, but something about owning my own place sounded perfect. Turns out that Mark skipped—or didn't even do—half of the required inspections on the place. I signed the document and suddenly found myself saddled with a building that needed major maintenance and a phone number for Mark that only seemed to get me to his voicemail."

"He stopped seeing you then?" Henrietta clarified.

"Yes. He dropped off the face of the earth, or so it felt like, and I found out through the grapevine that this wasn't the first time he'd done this."

"And he was still able to keep his realtor's license?"

"Yes. I mean in my case I signed the documents, I wasn't coerced in any way, at least no legally prosecutable way. I was stuck."

"What was the fallout for you?"

"Thousands of dollars and nearly six months past the slated open time," Sassy said matter-of-factly.

"I bet that made you angry."

She looked up and made eye contact with the detective. "It did. I'd be lying if I said it hadn't affected me, but just because I wasn't happy with how things turned out didn't mean I had reason to kill the man."

"From the way it looks you got your revenge."

Sassy flinched. "I didn't even know Mark was coming to the tasting."

"What did you say to him when he showed up?" Henrietta asked.

"I asked him what he was doing here and he said it was to see how I was doing. Something I didn't believe for a second. I mean, I got the "Best Business" award two years ago and I heard nothing from him. But he wouldn't admit to any other reason."

"Did you have cause to believe there could be another reason?"

"No," she said then frowned. "I mean, I felt like there was though by the way he avoided answering my questions. I mostly wanted to point out to him how ironic, in a terrible way, it was for him to show up like he had but he just kept saying he was there for the tasting."

"I see," Abe made a note in his notebook.

"You hadn't seen him before last night?" Henrietta asked.

"No."

Henrietta turned to look at Abe. "It seems to me that there was no way she could have planned for this to happen."

Abe finished making his note then looked up, first at Sassy then letting his gaze land on Henrietta. "I hate to be the bearer of bad news, but we don't tend to bring people into the station unless there is…evidence."

"What evidence?" Sassy asked.

"My officers found your prints on the chilies that were placed in Mr. Wharton's chocolate and—"

"That was in everyone's chocolate," Sassy interrupted.

"Miss Roberts," Abe said more forcefully, "It was a different chili than the ones in the rest of the chocolate. The specific kinds that Mr. Wharton was allergic to."

Sassy's mouth hung open but she didn't say anything.

"You're saying that only his chocolate was laced with a certain pepper?" Henrietta clarified.

"Yes. It looks very...deliberate."

"But how..." Sassy shook her head. "I had those chocolates made up the night before. They were all laid out in a specific order for the seating because I did have a few nut allergies to contend with. I used markers to indicate the specific plates."

"What was Mark's marker?" Henrietta asked.

"I just used an M. I had to write it out on a spare card because he was an add-in."

"She had no way of knowing he was coming," Henrietta said to Abe.

"That's not the way it looks to us."

"I...I think I might need a lawyer," Sassy said, swallowing hard. "I've told you the truth but...it doesn't seem like it's enough."

"I'll go get you that lawyer," Abe said, standing up. He left them and Henrietta reached over and placed her hand on top of Sassy's.

"We'll get to the bottom of this."

"Henrietta, I honestly don't know what happened. I mean, did someone come in and add that chocolate to the mix? Someone who knew he was coming?"

Henrietta thought back to Sassy's kitchen. There was a backdoor and it was possible...it just seemed so improbable.

"I don't know, but like I said, we'll get to the bottom of this."

Sassy met her gaze and nodded. "Thank you."

Henrietta didn't respond, knowing that there was nothing else to say, but she knew for a fact that she and Ralph would have more on their plate than just searching for Calvin. Henrietta thought of what her sister had said and felt her stomach clench. She couldn't tell her friend she wouldn't help her, but she also didn't want to let her sister down. She was confident in her own abilities to multitask, at least with regard to the two cases she now found herself mixed up in, but could she convince her sister of the same?

---

"PASTRAMI ON RYE WITH THE WORKS," Ralph said to the man behind the sandwich counter.

"You got it," he replied then looked to Henrietta.

"Turkey, lettuce, tomatoes, mayo, and cheddar cheese on wheat, please."

"These'll be up in a few minutes."

Henrietta and Ralph walked over to where a rack of chips was set up and made their selections and then Henrietta grabbed an unsweetened iced tea from the fridge before they went to sit down awaiting their sandwiches.

"So, she's under arrest on suspicion of murder, huh?" Ralph asked.

"It looks that way."

"That's crazy. Sassy couldn't hurt a fly."

"You and I both know that, but someone's doing a good job of making it look otherwise."

"Who?" Ralph asked, munching on a crunchy chip. "I mean, does Sassy even have enemies?"

"I asked her that actually, but she couldn't think of one person."

"Odd." Ralph leaned back in the bench seat and rubbed at his jaw.

"Are you ever going to shave again?" she asked, indicating his jaw.

"What? You don't like the rugged look?" he said with a grin. "I guess I got used to it in Virginia."

She rolled her eyes and then waited for her next comments until the man had delivered their orders.

"Ralph, I'm worried that there is more to this than meets the eye."

"You don't say."

His sarcasm rubbed her the wrong way. "No need for that," she said with a disapproving look.

"Sorry, it just irritates me that it's obviously a set up but facts are facts. As a detective you have to go with where the clues lead and right now they are a neon sign pointing to Sassy."

Henrietta bit into her sandwich and nodded in reply.

"I've got Scott running with this guy—Mark Wharton—and that might give us some insight."

"I talked to him this morning," she admitted.

"Huh?"

"Oh, Scott," she said, realizing he thought she meant Mark, "I asked him to look into Wharton as well."

Ralph grinned. "Great minds."

"He hasn't come back with anything yet?"

"Nope," Ralph admitted. "Still hacking—er, looking into it. I think there's some heavy encryption which bothers me."

"It does seem a little too much for an underhanded, womanizing realtor."

Ralph's eyebrows went up and she filled him in on how he'd treated Sassy.

"Sounds like the guy got what was coming to him."

"Careful," she admonished, "or Abe will think you're a suspect."

He chuckled. "But it doesn't sound good for Sassy. There's got to be more to this guy then. The encryption, the double accounts, the sleaziness of him. Yeah, this stinks."

She agreed and took another bite of her sandwich.

"Say, what about Calvin?" Ralph asked.

"What do you mean?"

"We promised your sister we'd look into it."

"And we will—are. I mean, isn't Scott looking into the email and phone number you got?"

Ralph looked sheepish.

"What is it?"

"I kind of got him working on the Wharton guy and

then the police needed his help on a few other cases and...he's booked."

Henrietta leaned back with a sigh. "I promised Clementine that we were working on it."

"Well, I *did* go to Virginia on her behalf."

"And on my dime," Henrietta pointed out with a smirk.

"True. But what about the kid?"

She frowned. "Which one?"

"Jacob. Why don't we get him on the email and number?"

Henrietta considered this. While she had come to trust the notes, she'd received from A Concerned Fellow Sleuth, even though they were written in anonymity, now that she knew he was behind it all she had started to view him slightly differently. He was young, a kid as Ralph said, and there was something of arrogance about him at times.

He wanted to join the private investigation team they had, and he wouldn't take no for an answer. She'd had to promise quite a bit to him in order to get him to share what he'd found. But still, as much as she wasn't certain he could handle full-time investigative work, she did know that he was gifted with computers—almost to Scott's level.

"I suppose we could ask him."

"You think he'll help without blabbing about it to his online buddies or whatever?" Ralph said.

She grinned. "That I can't be sure of. I do feel like

he's got to learn a bit more about the private investigation ethic, but we're up a creek without a paddle if we can't have someone look into the email and number."

"And he was able to trace the previous email."

"True. I'll talk to him today—he's working this afternoon."

"Good, keep me posted about what he says. I'll put a little muscle on him if he refuses."

Henrietta laughed. "You will not, but thanks for the offer, even if it's lip service."

Rather than deny it, Ralph merely grinned and took a too-large bite of his sandwich.

Henrietta slipped into thought. She needed a better fix on Calvin's location, if nothing more than to tell her sister they were close, but she also needed to make sure that Jacob didn't have some ulterior motive. It seemed unlikely. He'd been very straightforward about what he wanted. He wanted in on the action, as he put it, and he wanted to be part of their team, but she had to lay the ground rules. He had to do the leg work.

Still, there was only so much she could require of the young man before she started using him instead of training him.

Rummaging in her purse, she pulled out the slip of paper that Ralph had given her. It held Calvin's new telephone number and email address left at his former place of employment. It could all be fake, but they wouldn't know until someone looked into it and she wasn't willing to wait until Scott was free.

She had to prove to Clementine that she really was on the case and that it was going to have results. She had to find her nephew before whatever bad news that was following him caught up to him.

## 6

JACOB SAT at the desk behind the computer when Henrietta came back from lunch.

"Hey Henrietta," he said with a smile.

"Good afternoon, Jacob."

"Have a good lunch?"

She nodded, then trailed her finger along the countertop where the computer sat. Part of Henrietta wanted to trust Jacob. After everything they'd been through, finding out that his father was actually one of Henrietta's close friends who had died, and now knowing that he lived with his grandmother in an estate that Henrietta used to consult with for antiques purchases—there was a lot of history between them.

And yet Jacob was still only twenty-three and acted his young age at times. He was arrogant about his skills and determined to 'work with' Henrietta on a case, or several if he was allowed.

As she tried to understand her feelings toward the young man, he spoke up.

"Henrietta," he began, his gaze downcast. "I wanted to apologize."

"Oh?" She waited for him to explain.

"Yes. I think—no, I know—that I was out of line to make the demands I did and to overexaggerate the truth. I mean, to be fair, we do call it 'meeting up' online, but I should have realized Clementine would take that to be literal. And, perhaps if I'm even more honest, I wanted you all to think I was crucial to this case."

"And why is that?"

"Ever since I was young, I wanted to become a detective. Because of wanting to find my dad. I read cheap crime books and even a lot of The Hardy Boys," he chuckled. "A sorry excuse for a true education but we didn't have much, mom and I."

"It must have been difficult."

"I don't say it for that," he was quick to assure her. "I just meant that, along with those books I relied on I was very perceptive. I caught things that others didn't, and I thought, I have a gift for this. You know?"

"I understand," she said, and she did. She too was extremely observative and had used those skills for solving crimes in her recent history.

"I just thought that I could help. When I started helping you as the Sleuth, I thought this was my chance to prove to you I was worth working with. I see now I went about it the wrong way."

"You were helpful," she admitted. Her words brought a small smile to his lips.

"I'm glad for that, but I don't want to get in the way. I just...I wanted you to know I'm sorry and that I'll do whatever I can to help with Calvin, but I'm not going to demand anything."

Henrietta allowed a genuine smile to emerge. While she still thought he had much to learn, she appreciated his honesty and willingness to apologize. It also made what she had to ask that much easier.

"I'm glad you feel that way. I have a job for you."

"You do?" His shock was evident.

"Yes. You see, I've found myself involved with something a little more local and—"

"The murder at the tasting?" he blurted.

"I see you've read the papers."

"Well, they speculated it was murder and I only assume, since you were there, that there's more to the story."

"There is."

"Do you need help with that?" he asked.

"No, not yet at least. I do need help with a new email and phone number we got for Calvin when Ralph was in Virginia."

"A *new* email?" he asked.

"Yes. I know you've communicated with him before, but I'm going to ask you to refrain from that at this point. I'd like to send an email to my nephew, something we haven't tried yet, and see if we can get a response. Is there a way to trace my email to him or his back to me?"

He thought for a moment. "There's a way, but I don't know that I'd call it a trace exactly. I can look into it though. But the phone one could be trickier. Without police involvement it's hard to gain access to phone records and such."

"Does that mean you can't?"

He grinned. "I didn't say that."

"Then I don't want to know," she said with a laugh. "Here." Handing him the paper with the phone number and email on it. "Please let me know when I can send the email to him."

"You got it! And Henrietta?"

"Yes?" she said, turning to him before heading up to her rooms on the top floor of the large Victorian that housed her shop.

"Thank you. For understanding but also for still, you know, using me."

She smiled. "You're doing us a favor so thank *you.*"

He ducked his head just as the front bell rang out. They both turned toward the sound of heavy footsteps coming down the hallway toward them. When Ralph appeared Henrietta couldn't hide her surprise.

"What are you doing here?"

"Thought we might go down and look at the scene of the crime," he said with wagging eyebrows.

"You got us in?"

"I did," he said.

"Then by all means," she extended a hand. "Lead the way."

---

THE SCENT of chocolate still hung in the air even a few days after the tasting.

"Mmmm," Ralph said.

"No, you can't eat the evidence," Henrietta chided.

"Wouldn't dream of it, but I could go for some hot chocolate right about now."

The day had turned colder than Henrietta had anticipated as well, but her focus was on the crime scene and what they could find there. They wouldn't be allowed to touch anything, naturally, but Ralph's cop buddy let them in and said they had ten minutes to look around.

"Should we start in the kitchen?"

"Yep." Ralph followed her through the front of the shop, through the area where they'd all sat, and to the kitchen. "Did you notice anything when you came back to talk to Sassy?"

Henrietta thought back to that night. Sassy had been in the corner. She turned to stand exactly where she had been and closed her eyes to remember. Sassy had been facing away from Henrietta and turned quickly when she entered. Her back had stayed to the corner, but was that due to her hiding something or had she merely stood there?

Then Henrietta turned her head, eyes still closed. She saw the back door as it had been when she came in. The blinds were drawn and the lock had been turned vertical. Her eyes popped open. She walked toward the door now and noticed the lock was horizontal.

Using her sleeve to cover her hand she gently pressed down on the handle.

"What are you—"

"It's locked."

"I'd hope so. This is a crime scene."

"I distinctly remember glancing at the door when I came in. I'm positive the lock wasn't engaged."

"You're saying someone could have come in and changed out those chocolates?"

"When I came in, Sassy had the chocolates all out as she'd told me. They were in a specific order so she wouldn't give someone something they were allergic to."

Ralph made a sound that was a mix between a laugh and a cough. "Not funny, but that's exactly what happened."

"I know, but it would have been so easy for someone. I mean, she had them laid out and they even had little cards." Henrietta pointed to the cards that were still on the stainless-steel counter near the door.

Ralph bent low. "Huh. Here's Wharton's card right

here." He indicated the card with a finger and Henrietta bent down.

"What's that behind it?"

"Looks like an A?"

"But the M is written over it. Odd."

A cop moved into the doorway. "You two almost done?"

"May I open the back door?" Henrietta asked.

"Uh," he looked between her and Ralph. "Why?"

"I'll cover my hand," she said, showing him how her sleeve could go over her hand. "I just wanted to see something about the door."

He looked to Ralph this time who said, "She's harmless, I promise."

Henrietta shot Ralph a look but then turned back to the policeman.

"Fine," he said, "but don't touch it or rub it with your sleeve. I'm sure it's been dusted already but I don't want to take any chances."

"Thanks Charlie, appreciate it," Ralph said.

The man shrugged. "Come out when you're done."

"We'll be there in a minute." Ralph turned to Henrietta. "What are you doing?"

She gently unlocked the door with her sleeve covered hand and then opened it. It swung inward soundlessly. Then she stepped to the side and examined the hinges.

"Oiled," she said, frowning.

"You think someone oiled the hinges because they

knew they'd come in to switch out the chocolate?"

"It looks that way," she said, closing and locking the door. "Come on, we need to go talk to Sassy."

He followed her outside before asking his next question. "Hold on though, you've forgotten one thing."

"What's that?" she asked, waiting for him to unlock his truck.

He did and they climbed inside. "No one knew about Sassy's plan for the spicy chocolate at the end."

Henrietta nodded. "I've thought of that."

"And?"

"I don't have an answer."

"Well then," Ralph said sarcastically as he pulled away from the curb.

Henrietta shrugged. "I'm not saying I know *how* all this happened, but I think I can safely assume Sassy did *not* poison her former boyfriend and realtor, no matter how badly he treated her."

"I can agree with that. Sassy's a good person, but we need evidence, not character witnesses."

"I agree," Henrietta said, slipping into silence as they drove toward the police station.

She couldn't account for how someone could have known about Sassy's chocolate tasting plans nor could she pinpoint who had oiled the hinges on the back door, but she was fairly certain it was all an elaborate plan to frame Sassy.

Now, the question wasn't so much how but why? Why Sassy?

## 7

---

"OILED?" Sassy leaned back in the stiff chair of the interrogation room. "I have no idea. I mean, they were really squeaky a few weeks ago, I just remember because it was near silent in the front room but a woman and her small baby had come in to be out of a sudden downpour. I told them to have a seat and relax and the baby fell asleep, so when I went to take the trash out, I remember cringing it was *that* bad."

"But you don't remember when the noise disappeared?"

"No." She sighed. "It's like a rock in your shoe. You know when it's there but when it goes away you don't think about it again."

Henrietta smiled. "Good analogy and I know what you mean. But someone must have had access to oil it."

"I'm not in the habit of leaving—" she stopped short as if she'd remembered something.

"What?"

"So, I do remember a woman coming in the other day. Really elegant, you know? Poised? Anyway, I had been running around like a mad woman and my stomach wasn't feeling well," she made a face, "this lady looked at me as if she knew I wasn't feeling well and told me to run to the restroom, that she'd look after the shop. It was so bizarre but I was *not* feeling well so I did. I was gone for almost ten minutes," she looked down, heat fanning over her cheeks. "I mean, that's the only time my shop's been unattended, in a way."

"What did the woman look like?" Henrietta pressed.

"I don't know. Tall, blonde hair, stylish like I said. She had this…I don't know, *knowing* look. It was kind of freaky."

Henrietta grew very still and looked over at Ralph who was clearly thinking the same thing she was. The woman Sassy described sounded a lot like Anita Black, a woman Henrietta had had several run-ins with in the past.

"What? Do you know her?"

"In a way. But you think she could have oiled the hinges?"

"Aside from my delivery guy she's the only one that was in the kitchen."

"In the kitchen?" Ralph asked.

"Yeah, I came out of the bathroom to see her coming from the kitchen. She just smiled and said she was looking around. At the time I believed her. I mean, who wouldn't want to see what was behind the counter."

"Was your list for the tasting out?" Henrietta asked, taking a chance.

"My list? Oh, like a planning list? Nope. I keep that at home in my office."

"And you're positive that no one could have known about what you were serving? You didn't tell anyone? Maybe your delivery guy because of supplies you needed?"

"No. No one. I mean, I didn't want to risk it getting out so I kept it to myself and my own planning while I —" Sassy stopped and met Henrietta's gaze. "I just thought of something."

"What?" Ralph rushed to ask.

"I might have told Gina."

Henrietta leaned back in her chair. That was a new development. Gina was also a friend and there was no way she would have knowingly been involved in any scheme to hurt someone, but had she somehow unknowingly mentioned the special menu item?

"I'll talk with her, see if she remembers mentioning it anywhere."

"How could I have forgotten that?" Sassy dropped her head into her hands. "I wanted her to know about the coffee ones so that she could expect some feedback and then I let slip my idea for the last chocolate. I know it's not a new idea, but I thought I'd found a way to make the chocolate 'warm' without it being overpowering. I was really proud of it."

"And rightfully so," Henrietta said, comfortingly. "It was delicious and just the right amount of heat."

She looked up, tears in her eyes, and smiled at Henrietta. "Thank you."

"I don't like spicy and I liked that chocolate."

Now Sassy grinned. "I think you just like chocolate, Ralph."

He shrugged. "That may be true."

A knock followed by a young officer sticking his head in the room. "I'm afraid time's up."

Sassy immediately looked depressed, but Henrietta assured her that they would be back to talk to her and that they were working on this as best they could.

"Thank you," she said, smiling back at them both despite the tears in her eyes.

They left and Henrietta turned to Ralph once they were out of the station. "I need to go talk to Gina."

"You know she wouldn't have said anything on purpose."

"Of course not," Henrietta agreed, "but she might have said something in passing accidentally. I mean, if that really was Anita Black who offered to watch the shop then this could be much bigger than we'd anticipated."

Ralph nodded. "I'll drop you by Gina's and go check on Scott. I assume he'll have something concrete soon if not already."

They parted ways outside of Espresso Yourself, Gina Russo's coffee shop, and Henrietta made her way inside the coffee scented shop. Henrietta inhaled deeply and made her way to the counter past a few costumers occupying round tables in the main area. Most had computers out and were typing away or clicking on social media sites.

"Henrietta, so good to see you," Gina said, coming from the back room and wiping her hands on a towel. "What can I get you?"

"I'd love a latte, but I also have a few questions to ask you."

Gina looked surprised but immediately willing. "Why don't I make this latte for you and then we can sit down for a few minutes. I'll have Emily cover the front."

"Sounds good."

Henrietta chose a small table furthest away from anyone else. When Gina approached with a latte in a ceramic mug, a tall, thin girl with stringy blonde hair came from the back to watch the counter.

"What's up?" Gina said, scooting her chair closer.

Henrietta took a sip of the coffee and enjoyed the rich smoothness before answering. "I was just in to see Sassy."

"Oh gosh, I'd heard about that. I'm seriously in shock. There is no way Sassy has done *anything*. She wouldn't hurt a fly."

"I agree," Henrietta said, taking another sip, "but she

did mention something that I wanted to talk to you about."

"Sure, of course. Anything I can do to help."

"For the tasting, we're starting to think that Sassy was framed."

"Wait, what?"

"Ralph and I are investigating alongside the police." It was a bit of a half-truth, but Henrietta didn't want to undermine the public's faith in local law enforcement. "We discovered that the man who died wasn't supposed to be there at the tasting, but since he was the only one affected by the last chocolate she served, we think he was targeted and whoever did this to him used Sassy to commit the crime."

"Oh my gosh, Henrietta this is horrible."

"I know. It's awful to think about," Henrietta admitted, "But as you can imagine, we're wondering how this could happen. And I don't just mean literally but logically."

Gina frowned. "What do you mean?"

"Sassy is adamant that her tasting list was secret. No one could have known about the last chocolate flavor being spicy. But, when I talked to her, she said she might have mentioned it to you."

Gina gasped, her hand covering her mouth. "Oh my gosh."

"Gina, it's all right," Henrietta reassured her friend, "I'm not blaming you for anything. I just need to know who you might have told, you know?"

Gina blinked and leaned back in her chair. "I mean, I didn't go blabbing it, I promise."

"No one is saying you did."

"I know. Sorry," She sighed. "I need a double-shot."

Henrietta smiled. "Just tell me what you remember."

"Okay, so I do remember Sassy telling me that she was keeping the tasting menu a secret but I needed to get an idea of the coffee to provide but also wanted to know if she was doing any coffee flavored chocolates, you know? Anyway, she ended up spilling the beans to me about the spicy chocolate. I was so excited for her because it's so out of her norm, you know?"

"Right. Did you happen to share this with anyone though?"

"I don't think—" Gina paused then leaned forward. "Oh gosh, I did. I totally didn't mean to though—"

"Who, Gina?"

"I don't know." Gina looked helplessly at Henrietta.

"What?"

"It was some lady. She came into the shop and ordered a mocha. She asked for the Mexican one you know and we started talking about coffee and then it transitioned to chocolate somehow. I thought of Sassy's tasting and told the lady about it. She really seemed to know a lot about chocolate."

"But how did you tell her about the spicy chocolate?"

Gina turned pale and looked at her hands clasped on the tabletop. "I didn't mean to. I mean, I *knew* it was a secret, but the woman finally admitted she worked for a big food magazine and I thought—wow, this could be Sassy's chance. You know she's been trying to get her shop featured for a long time now. I decided to tell her, in a little more detail, about what the tasting would involve. I thought it might draw interest for her to actually commit to go."

"And this included mentioning the spicy chocolate."

"Yeah," Gina dropped her head against her palm, elbow on the table. "I'm an idiot."

"No, you're not." Henrietta made sure Gina could see the truth in her eyes. "You had no way of knowing what would happen and from what I can tell, you were honestly trying to help out Sassy."

"I was," she said, nodding vigorously.

"Well, thanks for telling me all of this." Henrietta stood, finishing off the last of her latte. "Thanks for the coffee and Gina, don't worry. We'll get to the bottom of this."

"I hope so. I feel awful."

"It'll be okay," Henrietta reassured her.

Gina took Henrietta's mug and went back behind the counter, but not before Henrietta called to her. "I forgot to ask," Gina came closer, "what did this lady look like?" An image of Anita Black flashed, and she wondered if it would match Gina's description.

"Uh, stylish for sure," she said, scrunching up her nose, "had dark, almost black hair and was kind of short actually."

Henrietta's hopes fell at this description. There was no way it could be Anita then since height couldn't be altered that dramatically even when hair color could.

"Thanks," she said then waved goodbye.

Henrietta needed to share what she'd found with Ralph and hopefully she'd be able to hear Scott's debrief about who Mark Wharton really was.

AFTER HENRIETTA STOPPED by to talk to Olivia who was covering the shop that afternoon, she decided to drive over to see Ralph. When her phone rang in the car she pressed answer but paused before pulling out of the driveway when Clementine's voice filled the space.

"Hen- Henrietta?"

"Yes, Clem? What's wrong?"

"I—I haven't heard back from Calvin."

Henrietta closed her eyes for a moment. While she understood her sister's worry over her son and wanted to have compassion, she felt more and more like Clementine was only creating distractions when she called in an emotional state like she was.

"Calm down," she said, her tone even, "take a deep breath. Are you at work?"

"I stepped outside for a break. I just...I keep thinking about him and don't know where he is and—and I want to talk to him. To ask him to forgive me and—"

"Clementine," Henrietta's voice was stern but gentle, "you need to stop this guilt."

"How?" her sister said, her voice breaking.

"You're doing everything you can, as are we, to contact him. Until he either replies to us or we gain more information from what Ralph brought back there isn't anything else we can be doing."

Clementine was quiet for almost a full minute before she spoke again. "I guess you're right."

"Is everything all right with you and Dan?"

Clementine gasped. "How...how did you—"

"I know that you want to find Calvin and his absence has been hard on you, but this seems...like more."

"We had a fight last night. I'm pretty sure he feels like I think he's not doing enough to find Calvin and... it wasn't good."

"Have you said anything that could make him think that?"

When her sister didn't reply immediately Henrietta let a gentle sigh escape. "I suggest you apologize to Dan after work. He's been helping when he can and I believe one of his biggest efforts is keeping you calm." Henrietta cringed, hoping her sister wouldn't hear that as an insult.

"You're right."

Henrietta let out another silent breath.

"I am a mess right now."

"It's understandable," Henrietta said, though she

cringed slightly because her sister was close to the 'too much' line as of late. "But don't take it out on your friends."

"Ouch," Clementine said, but a soft laugh came across the car speakers. "You're right. I'm sorry, Etta. I just…the not knowing is driving me crazy."

"I suppose in my line of work you find that waiting is very important."

"Detective work?"

"No, antiques," Henrietta said with a laugh. "And also, in detective work."

Clementine sniffed and cleared her throat. "Okay, I'm going to go. But thanks for hearing me out and calming me down. You're the best sister."

"Talk to you later," Henrietta said as she ended the call.

The line went silent and Henrietta took a deep, cleansing breath. Since when had things become so complicated? Then again, nothing about family was ever easy, was it? Not that it was bad, but it was something you learned to live with and cherish even. The quirks and flaws of her sister were coming out now, but Henrietta knew she had her own. It was a testament to her good friends and her sister that they dealt with her.

Henrietta smiled and put the car in drive. She made it to the Gershwin Private Investigators office in less than ten minutes and parked in the back, using her key to enter through the back door.

"Hello?" She called out.

"Henri?" Ralph's voice responded. "In here."

She found him and Scott in his office off the hall, Scott with his laptop on his knees.

"What took you so long?" Ralph asked, good naturedly.

"Good afternoon to you too," she said in response then relayed her sister's call in brief terms. "She's just dealing with a lot right now."

"Well, I don't have anything to contribute to that," Scott said, "But I do have some information on that guy you both asked me about."

"Which is why I'm here," Henrietta said, pulling a chair over.

"Sorry it took me so long," Scott said, looking between Henrietta and his father, "But it was like hacking into Fort Knox. Okay, so it wasn't that bad but he did have a *lot* going on."

"And what did you find out?" Ralph pushed.

"Right. Well, first off, he's done some shady things with his money, and he has a good amount of it. Money, that is." Scott listed off a few numbers in different accounts. "Besides that, I found that he used to work privately, running his own realty business, but a few years after he worked with Sassy, he quit."

"Do you know why?" Henrietta asked.

"Not exactly, but a few months later he started receiving payments from Deep Water Corporation."

"You've got to be kidding me," Ralph said, tossing up his hands.

"I know. They pop up everywhere these days, but I feel like it's a bear, stick reason."

"Excuse me?" Ralph gave Scott a confused look.

"Like you poke the bear, but you have to have a stick to do it."

Henrietta made a face. "Go on, Scott."

"Right. So, I'm not exactly sure what Mark was doing for DWC but he was getting paid well for it. And then I was able to find a few bills of sale for specific locations around town that he's been purchasing. I talked to a few of the sellers and it seems like he was doing it under the guise of purchasing for a larger corporation who has interest in setting up businesses in Heart's Grove."

"And people buy that?" Ralph said with incredulity.

"Why wouldn't they? They don't know that he's talking with other businesses. To them it would sound like a good thing, I'm sure." Henrietta shifted in her chair. "Did you find anything out about why he came to the tasting?"

"Not exactly. I did find some web browser history about him checking out the tasting, but other than that it seems like he just *wanted* to go."

"Scott," Henrietta said on a whim, "is there a way you can find out who was on the list for the tasting? Or perhaps those who had put in replies?"

He made a face. "Perhaps."

"Couldn't we just ask Sassy?" Ralph asked.

"Yes, but this will give us insight into who even asked questions versus who ended up attending."

"Here we go," Scott said and both Henrietta and Ralph turned toward him.

"That was fast," Ralph said.

"Sassy's security is, like, laughable. If she gets out of jail, I'll help her out."

"You mean *when*," Henrietta said.

"Right. Sorry—when she gets out of jail." He made a few more keystrokes and then leaned back. "Looks like who you told me about. There's an Angela and Tim, Leslie and Barbara, Ethel, and then another woman who made an inquiry. Anne McGill."

"A," Henrietta said to herself.

"Come again?" Ralph said, poking fun at her, knowing that she'd thought of something.

"The A on the card we saw in Sassy's kitchen. When I talked with Gina she said she'd spoken with a woman who was interested in the tasting. Someone who worked for a food magazine or something. She was the only person that Gina mentioned the special spicy chocolate to. She was just trying to help Sassy get some publicity but I think that this Anne woman may be more important than that."

"I'll look her up," Scott offered.

"Why didn't Sassy mention this Anne character to the police?" Ralph mused.

"I think I have the answer to that." Scott looked up.

"She sent in an email the day-of saying she couldn't make it and that she hoped someone could take her place. The rub? Sassy didn't open it."

"You're in her email?" Ralph frowned.

"It's the email associated with her website."

"She must have been too busy with preparations and running her shop to check it," Henrietta guessed.

"Still, she should have mentioned that to the police." Ralph didn't look happy. He never liked people who withheld things from the police.

"I'm sure she didn't do it on purpose or it hasn't yet come up in their questioning."

"Any good cop worth their salt would have been able to get that out of her if she were willing to share."

"And she may have already shared that with Abe and just not with us."

Ralph tossed up his hands again in defeat.

"All right," Henrietta said, standing. "I should get back to the shop but please let me know what you find out about this Anne woman. See if her magazine story is legitimate as well, please."

"You got it."

Ralph stood to walk her out and they parted ways with Scott who was likely going back to his bank of computers that were more powerful than a mere laptop.

"You think this all has to do with DWC, don't you?" Ralph said.

"Naturally," Henrietta admitted. "I mean, it would be too great of a coincidence for it not to."

"But how? How does this all fit?"

"I have no idea," she admitted. "On one side it would appear that Sassy got caught up with a man who now works for a corporation that is somehow out to interfere with this town, going so far as to blackmail the mayor." Henrietta shook her head, thinking about poor Mayor Lawrence and his run-in with the DWC. "But on the other hand, I wonder if it's not about Sassy at all."

"You think it's about *you?*"

"I hate to be so dramatic and self-focused but the thought has crossed my mind," Henrietta admitted. "Sassy is a good friend of mine. She was targeted. Is that to gain my involvement? Are they somehow hoping that I'll get wrapped up in this? And if I do, why would that matter?"

"Working for the DWC is quickly becoming a death sentence," Ralph mused. Then his gaze turned to her. "Henri, I don't like the thought of you involved in this. Maybe Scott and I should take it over and you can work full-time on Calvin's case?"

Her frown softened into a smile. "While I appreciate your care for my safety, I'm not backing down just because DWC is involved. If Anita Black has a hand in this then there is a reason behind it and we need to uncover that. Together."

Ralph let out a sigh. "All right. But promise me you'll be careful."

"When have I not?"

He rolled his eyes. "Don't make me count the times." Then he leaned forward and brushed a gentle kiss to her cheek.

She blushed and dipped her eyes, fumbling with her keys. "Have Scott call me when he knows what's going on."

"Of course," Ralph said.

Then Henrietta rushed out the back door. There seemed to be danger on all sides, not just from the Deep Water Corporation, but even the danger of falling further into this relationship with Ralph. Then again, not all danger was a bad thing.

## 8

HENRIETTA WALKED into the shop and was happy to see several couples searching through the different rooms which offered antiques from different time periods. Some rooms held a mix-match of decades but certain areas she'd decided to keep true to the period.

After answering a few questions from the customers and helping Jacob check them out and wrap the items, they found a break in the busyness to talk.

"Have you had any luck with the email or phone number?"

"Yes and no," he said, standing up to dust the nearby shelves with a feather duster. "I was going to call you because I wasn't sure if you were coming in to the shop today. I am ready for you to send that email."

Henrietta nodded. She'd already composed it and saved it in her email account but she wondered what it would all entail. When she asked, Jacob explained some of it but most of the words he used were not familiar to her.

"Suffice it to say," Jacob said, "we're adding some invisible...uh, text to your email. That's the best way I can think to explain it to you. The code will help me track where it goes and *should* send back information to me."

"Sounds like a good thing."

"You know what you're going to say?" His question, while slightly personal, had more of an informational bend to it, she knew.

"I've composed the letter, yes, but my hope is that —while we'll be able to track him—he'll come to us of his own accord. I do hope he knows we're searching for him for the sole reason of wanting to connect with him again. We're family and for someone who had no family up until I found Clementine, it's a wondrous thing to know there are more family members out there. If that makes sense."

Jacob smiled and nodded. "It does, as you know."

"Ah, true," she said with a smile. "I'm going to head upstairs for a little while. Should I send you the email I composed?"

"Actually, that's a good idea," he admitted. "We'll go ahead and send it from the work email so that it's attached to a knowable business. It may make Calvin feel more at ease to know that you're a real person with a website etc."

She nodded. "I'll forward it to you, and you can work your magic."

He smiled and said goodbye.

While Henrietta's body felt tired, her mind was twirling with the different aspects of what was turning into two very confusing cases. She stepped into her upstairs apartment and Sepia the cat rushed past her.

"Someone's hungry, aren't you?" she asked the cat.

When the Flame Point Siamese rushed to her bowl, Henrietta knew that her answer was yes.

"All right, here you go." She put a half a cup of dry food in the bowl, noting the cat's chagrin. At night, Sepia enjoyed a feast of wet food but during the day Henrietta stuck to a dry-food diet. It did seem to help keep the cat in shape even if it made her a bit disgruntled.

"Now don't look at me like that. I'm not one to give in, and you know it."

Sepia licked a paw then shot off the floor to walk on the table, likely looking for any scraps left behind. Henrietta ignored the feline and went about making herself a cup of tea.

She thought about what Sassy had said, the evidence they had found, and the reality that the Deep Water Corporation seemed to be a rather large player in this whole thing. But the question remained: why?

Why would someone from DWC want to kill Mark? It seemed clear, to Henrietta at least, that Anita Black had found a way into the kitchen and she was likely behind how they had killed Mark. Then again, why would Mark come to the tasting in the first place?

And then there was the woman named Anne. How did she fit into all of this? Was it possible that she'd been planning to attend but Mark took her place for some reason? It would be nearly impossible to know the answer to that question until they knew more about the woman, but Henrietta liked to mull things over when possible.

Sighing, she took her tea to her small living room and turned on a crime show. It was a silly excuse for early evening entertainment, but she wasn't ready for dinner nor was she ready to go to bed. She didn't even want to work on her book, which was most shocking of all since she'd finally finished it and was now going back through editing it.

Leaning back against the sofa, she allowed herself to think of the real reason behind her melancholy.

Calvin.

She wanted to find him, but she had a nagging feeling in the pit of her stomach that wouldn't let her believe he was missing by anything other than choice. And that reality made her wonder why.

Why had Calvin worked so hard to stay hidden? Did it have something to do with Clementine? Or perhaps Calvin's father and notorious mob boss, Ernie De Luca? It seemed most logical that he was hiding from Ernie, but after the trouble Henrietta had found herself in when she'd thought that Calvin had come to visit her but it turned out to be an imposter, she'd assumed that Calvin's father wasn't interested in him in any way. Her own research had proved that De Luca had several kids by several women and it seemed implausible that he'd care so much about a random son who seemed to want nothing to do with him.

Which brought her back to the why. Why wouldn't Calvin contact them? The thought was that he was in trouble, and if that were the case her email might help with that since she'd offered to help him out of that trouble, but would he believe her? Would he take her up on that? As she'd faced with the fake Calvin, having a nephew who only wanted a relationship for her money was not something she was interested in.

But if the *real* Calvin was in trouble, she would help if she could.

Balling up her fists, Henrietta forced her attention back on the show and Calvin out of her mind. She couldn't solve any of these mysteries without help and currently everyone helping her was busy doing just that, so she had to do what she'd told Clementine. Be patient!

---

THE NEXT MORNING Henrietta got a call from Scott. He tried his best to loop Ralph into the call but Ralph was having technical difficulties in addition to being at a diner with loud customers, so Scott gave up and called Henrietta back.

"I've got news on that Anne woman."

Henrietta's heart pounded a little faster. "Let's hear it."

She smiled, sitting up straighter at her kitchen table. She'd had a good dinner last night and gone to bed early. After deciding to let everyone do what they do best, she found a great sense of comfort in knowing that she'd done what she could and she could only wait.

"Turns out, she's not exactly who we thought she was."

Henrietta laughed. "I had a feeling. No one seems to be right now."

"True. So, it looks like she once did write for a food magazine in Seattle, but she hasn't done that in years. She lives in Heart's Grove though, ironically."

"Do you have her address?" Henrietta asked.

"Yes…" Scott sounded hesitant.

"Not to worry, I rarely go anywhere without your father."

That seemed to pacify him and he read off the address for her.

"What else did you uncover?"

"It seemed as if she really was going to go to the tasting and then canceled, but she's been living on an odd deposit I can't trace just yet."

"What do you mean?"

"It's not from something like social security or

anything like it, it's more like someone drops two thousand dollars into her account every month.

"And that's what she lives off of?"

"I can't find any other indication of a job or any form of income."

"Is it a bank transfer?" Henrietta asked.

"Yes, but I can't seem to trace it. Or at least, not fully yet. I'll have to let you know."

"All right. Well, it looks like I'll need to go have a talk with her."

"Henrietta," Scott said, his tone warning.

"I'll take your father, it's all right."

He chuckled. "Okay, as long as you promise."

"I do."

They said goodbye and she hung up. Standing, she began pacing and formulating a plan. Then, when she had it in place she called Ralph. He didn't answer but she left a message, telling him to meet her at Anne's house. She had no fear that an older woman would be too much of a threat to her. Still, she had promised Scott she'd bring Ralph and she'd left a message to make good on that promise.

Dressed for the cloudy day, she climbed into her Mini Cooper and set the GPS on her phone to take her to Anne's house. When she arrived, she didn't see Ralph's truck and called him again. This time, her call went straight to voicemail and she figured that either his phone was off or on silent. Still, she wasn't sure she wanted to knock on the woman's door without someone knowing where she was.

She shot him a text, including the address yet again, and waited.

After fifteen minutes without a response she called Scott but his phone went to voicemail too. Were they talking to one another?

Frustrated and impatient, Henrietta decided that Anne posed no threat to her. In fact, her suspicion was aligning itself with the thought that Anne was innocent in all of this. Perhaps someone who had signed up for the party and taking the last coveted place, she'd been bought out so that Mark could take her place.

It didn't answer the question of who had done that or how anyone else had found out about the last chocolate tasting menu item, but it seemed the most likely. Especially because she expected Scott would have told her of the woman's involvement in anything that seemed untoward. Something he hadn't found.

After one last call to Ralph, Henrietta stepped from her car, straightened her jacket, and headed for the front door.

The house was a modest cottage set on a hillside with a nice view of the water. The lawn was tidy with trimmed grass and sheered hedges, but the house itself boasted nothing special. The shades were drawn and the light on the front porch was off despite the darkness of the storm clouds overhead. If it had been light sensing she assumed it would have been on.

At the solid oak door, Henrietta lifted her hand and knocked. When the door slowly opened inward, Henrietta flinched. She hadn't expected that.

"Hello?" she called out, wondering if the woman had come inside and forgotten to close the door all the way. Her own back door had done that for several months before she'd gotten Ralph to fix it for her. "Hello? Anne McGill? Helloooo?"

When there was no answer to her call she turned around and looked up and down the street. She'd already taken notice of the cars in the general vicinity. None were occupied as if someone was watching the house. Then her eyes took in the houses next to her but the windows were empty, their occupants likely all at work.

"Hello?" she called again, but still there was no answer.

She checked her phone but there was nothing from Ralph. This was a situation she didn't relish, and yet if she suspected foul play wasn't it her duty to investigate?

She navigated to make a call, typing in 9-1-1 and hovering her finger over the buttons before she stepped inside the house.

The air was stale, as if the door or windows hadn't been opened in several days. The musty smell was soon followed by another smell Henrietta recognized. Decomposition. It wasn't so strong that it was overpowering, but it was distinct nonetheless.

Quickly moving into the main area of the room she looked around the corner and saw a body on the floor. Her gag reflex took over and she nearly threw up, but instead she backed away and rushed for the door, her finger jamming on the call button only to realize the screen had gone black with inactivity.

Outside, she drew in deep drafts of air and looked around. She was about to open her phone again to call when she caught sight of movement down the street. It was a woman in a brilliant red coat scurrying down the sidewalk toward a hiking path. Henrietta knew of these from her time living in Heart's Grove. Many of the neighborhoods had them. They wound from the neighborhoods through the dense foliage toward the beach or along the roads.

They were perfect for walkers, runners, and bikers since they followed nearly the same paths of the roads but yet without being near traffic.

"Stop," Henrietta called out. She felt foolish the minute she did, knowing the woman was too far away to hear her but also wondering how she was planning on making the woman stop. And, more than that, it wasn't as if she'd seen the woman coming out of the house. It was just the fact that, from this distance, it looked like Anita Black.

Henrietta moved quickly down the sidewalk toward the path, opening her phone and dialing the police as she did. The dispatcher answered with a characteristic unemotional response and through heavy breaths due to her increased speed following the possible Anita Black, Henrietta explained what she'd found.

"A dead body?" the dispatcher replied.

"Yes." Henrietta rattled off the address and tried to field the young woman's questions as best she could, while her lungs demanded more oxygen.

Finally, Henrietta reached the path and rounded the corner. The woman was still far ahead, but Henrietta felt as if she were gaining on her.

"Ma'am," the dispatcher said, "we'd ask that you not leave the area. It sounds like you're—are you running?"

"Yes," Henrietta gasped. "But I'm in pursuit of," more gasping, "a suspect." She felt foolish the minute she said it. What would she do if she did catch up with the woman? And she also didn't feel as if she had any right to use the cop language as she had, but it was the first thing that came to mind.

"Ma'am, that is not—wait, what suspect?"

"I'll need to call you back, Darla," Henrietta said, a pain in her side slowing her down even more. "Make sure you send the police. Preferably Detective Paige."

Henrietta hung up, shoving her phone into her purse swinging at her side. She was able to gain a little on the woman but then the red coat vanished from her sight around a corner and, when she rounded that same corner a few moments later, the woman was gone.

## 9

"Drat!" Henrietta said, gasping.

She waited a few moments, looking back and forth, wondering where Anita—or whoever it was—had gone to, but when she saw nothing she gave up. The walk back to Anne's house was slow going, her feet now hurting from the new boat-style shoes she'd gotten and hadn't yet worn-in.

When she came from the mouth of the path she saw that police cars and an ambulance were all in front of Anne's house. She slowly made her way toward where she saw the detective standing, talking with—Ralph!

"Now you decide to show up," she said, approaching both men and giving Ralph a look that showed she wasn't happy about his lack of communication with her.

"Henri, there you are. Thank God!"

"I'm fine, it's that body in there that you should be worried about."

Both men looked at her and in the absence of words, their looks said volumes.

"What?" she finally asked, not wanting to guess. Had there been even more bodies in there than Anne's?

"There is no body," Abe said.

"I—what?" Henrietta moved as if to go into the house but the detective gripped her arm lightly.

"I'm sorry, but you can't go in there. You *can* give me all the details of what you thought you saw though."

"Thought I...I didn't *think* I saw anything. I saw a woman's body on the floor. Cause of death was not readily apparent, but I didn't approach the corpse either. I came outside to call but then saw..." Here's where the story diverged from being in her favor.

"Saw what?" Ralph said.

"I thought I saw Anita Black."

"Who?" Abe said.

"It doesn't matter because she disappeared, but it was too much of a coincidence for me to see her leaving this area and then for me to have just found a body. I just...I had to go after her."

"And that's when you called in the body?"

"Yes," She said, thinking back to the timeline. "I think it might have taken me about four to five minutes from finding her and then calling it in."

"All right," Abe said, scratching that on his notebook.

"But I don't see how a body could be here one minute and then be gone the next?"

"They don't usually walk off," Abe said dryly.

"Really?" Henrietta said with equal sarcasm. "Honestly, Abe, have I ever been the woman to cry wolf?"

"No," he admitted, turning to look at the house. "Which is why we're investigating. It took us about ten minutes to get here which gives the possible killer almost a fifteen-minute head start to get the body out."

"You think it was removed?"

"Well, it didn't disappear," he said.

"True. Of course." Henrietta shook her head, wiping her brow which still had perspiration on it from her jog after the possible-Anita.

"I noticed the smell of chemicals when I walked in," Ralph admitted.

"You went inside?" Henrietta said.

He shrugged. I arrived just as the police were getting here. Paige took me in with him."

"On protest," Abe muttered.

"Smelled of chemicals and the place was clean."

"Fifteen minutes? That seems…impossible. I arrived and the door was open—I knocked and it opened, that is. I didn't try the handle, I promise." She made sure that Abe was writing down what had happened before she continued. "Then I went in and the smell was pretty bad. It was a mix of musty, no open windows, and…dead body."

Abe looked up at this.

"I know it's hard to believe, especially hearing Ralph said it smelled clean but…" she shrugged. "Is it possible there was a team waiting to clean the place?"

This time when Abe looked at her she knew what he was thinking. *You watch too much television.*

"I know it seems impossible but," she was hesitant to admit it to Abe because there was no proof, but it wasn't out of the realm of possibilities that the Deep Water Corporation was involved in this. They seemed to have money, motivation, and a whole lot of people in their pockets.

"If we step away from the theatrical, what else could account for what you saw?"

"I wasn't hallucinating if that's what you mean."

"Not saying that," he looked back at the house, "but there was nothing there, Henrietta."

Her shoulders slumped. This was beyond plausible and yet here she was, telling the head detective of Heart's Grove that she'd found a body and yet there was no body. It made no sense, she realized that, but then she had a feeling there was more here than what met the eye.

After filling Abe in on what Scott had said and why she was even there in the first place he assured her that they would go over the house with a fine-tooth comb. He too was worried about the fact they couldn't get a hold of Anne McGill who clearly wasn't home, so it amplified what they were doing, even if it wasn't to the level of a murder investigation. Then, concluding his questions, he sent Henrietta and Ralph on their way.

"I'm sorry I didn't answer," Ralph said as he walked her to her car.

"Me too," she admitted with chagrin. "I know it sounds impossible but I swear there was a body on the kitchen floor."

"I know," he said, resting a gentle hand on her shoulder. "I have a feeling she'll show up." He made a face that was mostly a grimace.

"I can't believe I couldn't catch up with Anita though."

"Or who you *thought* was Anita."

"True. But," she hesitated then looked up at Ralph. "I think she was luring me away from the house. They had to get the body out."

"But why would they leave it there in the first place then? If it was, as you say, a few days old, why bother moving it?"

"I don't know," she said. She lifted her hand and rubbed at her temple where a headache was starting. She needed water and to sit down and think.

"Hey, I'll take ya to lunch at the docks. Sound good?"

She almost said no, wanting to go home and sulk, but Ralph looked genuinely hopeful she'd come and she was hungry.

"I'll meet you there."

"You bet." He grinned and nodded, taking off for his truck.

She climbed in and it was only then that she saw the note on her windshield. Frowning, she pulled it out from under her wipers and sat back in her car to read it.

HENRIETTA,

*Stay away from me or I'll tell the police what you did.*
*-Anne*

---

HENRIETTA BROUGHT the note into the Bait and Tackle where she met Ralph at their favorite corner.

"What's that?" he asked, noticing her grim expression.

She slid into the seat across from him and slid it over. "I found this on my windshield."

"You've never met this Anne person, have you?"

"No. Of course not. The first time I saw her was...dead." She swallowed. "At least I'm fairly certain that the body was hers."

"Then where did this come from and how did it end up on *your* windshield?"

"I have no idea," Henrietta admitted. "I don't even know if she wrote it."

"More than that, what is she talking about?"

"I don't know that either," Henrietta admitted.

"Hold on," She flattened it out in front of her and frowned. "See this here, the part where it says my name?" She pointed to the paper.

"Yeah? So, what?"

"Look at the 'a' in "stay" and the 'a" in my name."

Ralph leaned closer and scrunched up his nose as he looked at both letters. "Different."

"Very different," she said. "I'm no handwriting expert, but I'd say that just because the a was at the end of a word wouldn't make it *that* much different than other a's would it?"

"That I can't tell you, but I think you'd better turn this in to Paige. He's gonna need to keep this as evidence."

Henrietta nodded. "I should have given it to him while I was there but I wanted you to see it and you'd already left."

"We'll go drop this off when we get done with lunch."

She nodded and they ordered. The clam chowder for Henrietta and fish and chips for Ralph, though Henrietta made sure to point out that he should also be ordering a salad. He merely laughed and continued to dip his breaded and fried fish in copious amounts of tartar sauce when their lunch arrived.

"So how do you think the DWC is involved in all of this? Or maybe the better question is why?"

"That is a good question," Henrietta said, dipping a

piece of her bread in the chowder. "I have no idea aside from the reality that Mark was working for them."

"There's got to be a thread tying all of these pieces together. Tell me this," Ralph wiped at his mouth with a napkin. "What is DWC's goal?"

"Goal?" Henrietta asked, her head tilting to the side.

"Yeah, what are they up to? What do they want?"

"If we think back to when Seamus died," she looked around the diner as if he might walk in at any minute but they both remembered his death and the case surrounding it, "it was all surrounding the ability to import and export to Canada without incurring any type of taxable income. But, on reflection, that couldn't have been their end goal."

"Why not?" Ralph asked. He likely had his own opinions but wanted to hear what she had to say.

"It's too…petty. A big corporation like that would have other ways around those things. Perhaps it was *what* they wanted to smuggle, not so much why they were doing it."

"All right, so then what is that all about?"

"If we knew, would we be in this predicament?"

He grinned, shoving a fry covered in ketchup into his mouth. "Probably not."

"All right, what about this," Henrietta said, warming to the subject, "Mark worked in real estate, right?"

Ralph nodded.

"So, what was he doing before he came to the tasting?"

"Do you mean *right* before or—"

"No, like for work. He was acquiring buildings in Heart's Grove."

"Oh, right. For his 'employer'."

"Which we can assume is DWC." When Ralph nodded she continued. "What if they are behind purchasing those buildings for a reason. I mean, clearly whatever they are doing is centered in Heart's Grove and they tried to wrap Mayor Lawrence into their trap by blackmailing him. Is there something they know about Heart's Grove—something profitable—that they are after?"

"If we knew that, I don't think we'd be sitting here trying to figure it out."

"Good point," Henrietta said. Then she thought of Sassy. "And my next question is even more curious."

"Which is?"

"Why Sassy? If they wanted to kill Mark for some unknown reason, why do it in Sassy's shop. I'd thought it was to get back at me, but what if there was another reason?"

"I feel like only Sassy would have that information," Ralph said.

"I should go speak to her again," Henrietta agreed. "When I drop off this note I'll see if I can talk to her. Maybe there's more about Mark she didn't tell us—or forgot to mention."

Ralph shrugged. "Love is a funny thing."

"You think she's protecting him—or his memory—by not sharing?"

"I don't know if it's so much that or she is not thinking clearly about it all."

"She didn't seem *that* broken up about his death," Henrietta pointed out.

"Good point," Ralph said. "Maybe it's more about her then, and not him."

"How so?" Henrietta asked.

"We tend to protect ourselves, don't we? Especially if it's an embarrassing or shameful thing. Press her a little, see what she might be hiding."

While Henrietta didn't like the thought of pressing her friend while she was in jail, she needed the truth more than she needed to make Sassy comfortable.

"I will," she admitted, looking down at the note one more time. She needed to give that to Abe and she needed to figure out why she'd been targeted, because now more than ever she felt as if something was coming—like a storm brewing on the horizon, she needed to prepare for bad weather. No matter what form it took.

## 10

HENRIETTA DROVE to the police station, thinking about everything that had happened and wondering what was going to come about next. If it had been Anita Black she'd seen, she wondered what she would have been doing at Anne's home?

And the other thing she couldn't reason was why whoever had killed the poor woman—for she was dead, Henrietta knew that much—had left her there and not taken her body before?

She pulled into a parking space a block from the station but pulled her phone from her bag before she left, checking her messages. There was one text from Olivia asking about a specific painting and its authentication papers, which Henrietta replied to immediately, and then there was an email from someone she didn't recognize.

Opening the app, she saw that the email address

was unfamiliar to her and had several letters and numbers in it as if it had been a randomized address or something similar. The subject section had also been left blank.

At first Henrietta didn't want to open it. She knew better than to open links or to download from unfamiliar email addresses, but could opening an email be just as bad?

While she was waiting, thumb hovering over the email, a car alarm went off a few cars over making Henrietta jump. Her thumb hit the screen and the email popped open. When she saw who was writing her she felt as if it had been an act of God to make her open that email because it was from Calvin.

She rushed through the short email and leaned her head back against the seat. In so many words he'd all but asked her to stop looking for him. He wanted his space and he couldn't come back to them. At least not yet.

She read it several more times, trying to read between the lines. Was what he was saying the truth, or was he saying it in case the email was intercepted?

Biting her lip, she nearly called Jacob right then and there, but something held her back. She needed to speak to Jacob in person, to see what his reaction was and to see what his suggestions for figuring out where the email originated from—if he could do such a thing. She always preferred doing things in person anyway and now would be no exception.

Putting her phone away, she straightened and went into the station. The receptionist, recognizing her by now, waved her through to the back and to Abe's desk. She called ahead and Henrietta could see the moment Abe looked up to meet her gaze, expecting her arrival.

"Good afternoon, Miss Hewitt," he said with a tired smile. "Surprised to see you again so soon."

"Yes, well," she adjusted her purse strap then pulled it off her shoulder. "I found something on my car I felt I needed to give you."

Abe frowned as she handed over the note scribbled on yellow legal paper. He read it, for what Henrietta took to be several times, before he looked up to meet her gaze. "Where did you say you got this?"

"It was stuck under my windshield wiper when I went to leave the crime scene."

"And you didn't call me over?" His expression was pained, and Henrietta felt the pang of regret you get when you know you've made a mistake.

"I should have. I realize that now, but I wanted to show Ralph and..."

"Henrietta," Abe looked down at the note and then back at her. "This looks bad."

She nodded, not needing him to spell it out for her.

"I wish you would have left it and come to get me. It would have established that you didn't take this from the house—"

"I didn't."

"*I* know you didn't, but we have no proof of that. If

you had taken it from the house and the body was there and is now gone…it doesn't look good."

"Why in the world would I call the police to a crime scene if I altered it? That makes no sense."

"I'm not saying it makes sense, exactly, it's just…" he pointed to the note laying on his desk now. "I'm going to need to take this into evidence."

She nodded then pointed at the top without touching the paper. "If you'll note, it doesn't look like my name is written by the same hand."

He met her gaze. "So, you're a handwriting expert now?" His words were partly joking but she could tell he was exasperated. And he had a right to be. She knew better.

"No, just observant. Look at the a's."

He did for a full minute before looking back at her. "I'll get a handwriting expert on this but…I'm going to have to ask you not to leave town."

She laughed, "You really think—" then sobered when she saw his serious expression. "I wouldn't leave town during an investigation anyway."

"Good."

"May I speak with Sassy?" she asked, knowing that the woman was still being held in the small jail area instead of being taken to the county jail in Port Angeles. It was a blessing but also troubling her friend was incarcerated in any fashion.

"Yes," he finally said. "Only fifteen minutes."

"That'll be plenty."

He left to set up the meeting and finally, ten minutes later, she was seated across from her friend. After asking how she was doing though the action seemed slightly fruitless, she got down to business.

"Sassy," she said, edging her words with compassion, "I need you to be completely honest with me."

"Of course, Henrietta." She looked slightly offended but Henrietta didn't have time to assuage her friend's feelings.

"What else is there about Mark? What aren't you telling me? Telling the police?"

Her face paled and she looked down at her hands, shackled to the table.

"I—it's embarrassing, Henrietta."

"It may very well be," she said, her words gentle, "but is it worth keeping to yourself if you go to jail for his murder?"

That brought the woman's head up. "No. You're right." She took in a deep breath and, dropping her gaze, explained, "when we were together I shared with him how important the shop was to me. That it was a lifelong dream, you know? Something that I couldn't believe had happened."

"That's understandable," Henrietta agreed.

"After a week or so he started playing hard ball—as he said. He claimed he hated to do it but that he had to. He was getting pressured by his clients. I had no idea what he meant but he said I'd see." She shivered and bit her lip before continuing, "Then I got an email that night with a list—a fake list—of health code violations."

"What? How did he manage that?" Henrietta asked.

"I didn't reply right away. I mean, I honestly considered ignoring him and hoping—praying—he'd go away, you know?"

Henrietta nodded.

"But then he kept after me saying he was going to release these to the public. My shop would be ruined. He even said he had a health inspector that would validate the claims."

"How was that possible? There would have to be a way to challenge the findings. To have another inspection or something?"

She shrugged, looking hopeless. "Sure, that's true, but the damage would be done. I mean, I was gearing up to be featured in a few bigger name magazines in Seattle. I was really trying to make Sassy's Sweets become a tourist destination. Anything even hinting at health code violations would have been enough to shut down any of those articles." Tears were coursing down her cheeks now and she reached to wipe them away accompanied by the clinking sound of her handcuffs.

"I'm so sorry, dear," Henrietta said. "I can only imagine the situation you were in, but did you consider talking to the police?"

"This is so foolish, I know, but I was so busy I just... didn't." Now Sassy looked hopeless, as if she didn't have any way out of the situation she'd found herself in. "I was busy getting ready for the tasting and Mark said he was going to be out of town for the week so he would expect an answer when he came back."

"You must have been even more shocked than I realized to see him at the tasting then."

"I was. I didn't let it show, but I was completely shocked. I wondered if he had to have an answer soon and I didn't know what I was going to do. Don't you see, Henrietta?" she said, her eyes pleading.

"See what, Sassy?"

"See that I couldn't tell the police this? I mean, it sounds terrible and like a good reason to k-kill him. I didn't—I swear I didn't—but I know how it looks."

"Looking like one thing and the reality of another are two separate things, dear." Henrietta took a deep breath and considered the reality of what she was hearing. Mark was motivated to purchase the shop, she assumed for the Deep Water Corporation, but why?

"Did he mention why it was so important that he got *that* specific location? I mean, there are many buildings around yours. Why pick a shop that was already filled with equipment and things like that?"

"I'm not sure. He made it sound like they wanted *that* building and another wouldn't do. Now I'm wishing I'd just agreed."

"Who else would want to kill him then," Henrietta said, though the question was more for herself than Sassy.

"I have no idea. Maybe his boss because he couldn't

deliver? I don't know—I mean, Mark was an unscrupulous guy, I get that, but I have a hard time believing he would have turned in those threatening papers."

"You think?'

"Maybe I'm just trying to think better about him now since he's gone."

They talked a few more minutes, Henrietta trying to direct the conversation to something aside from death and murder, but by the end she was too lost in thought to be much company to the incarcerated woman.

"I'll come again," she promised Sassy when the officer came to escort her out.

But first, Henrietta reasoned, she needed to find out what was so special about the sweet's shop that DWC was willing to kill for it—assuming they were behind Mark's death.

## 11

---

THE SUN SHINING through the filmy curtains of her bedroom woke Henrietta right before her ringing phone. It was startling to be woken lazily from sleep only to have the silence shattered by a call, but Henrietta pushed from bed and reached her phone in time to see it was Detective Paige calling.

For some reason, seeing his name on the caller ID made Henrietta's insides clench. She had done nothing wrong—aside from taking the note from her car windshield before she should have—so why did she feel as if the law was out for her?

"Hello?' she said, pressing the answer button.

"Good morning, Henrietta," Abe said. "I'm sorry to call so early but we've found...well, a body was found on the beach. Can you come down to Pike's Point to see if it's the same one you saw in the house?"

This was the furthest thing from the news she'd

expected to get from his call but her mind quickly cleared. "Yes, I'll be there in fifteen minutes."

"Thanks." He hung up without further information and she set the phone down to get dressed.

She grabbed a granola bar and a bottle of water on her way out the door and shot a text to Olivia before starting her car. She hated to call the young woman in since she hadn't been feeling well, but it was either her opening the shop or it would remain closed until Henrietta could come back to open. Jacob was at a class that morning at a community college nearby so he couldn't step in on late notice either.

The drive to Pike's Point was simple and Henrietta found she'd arrived in ten minutes, not the fifteen she'd promised. While she likely didn't look as put together as usual she was less worried about appearances in the wake of a dead body.

She approached the gathering of officers and felt her stomach clench. She'd been to a scene like this before but in the hills on the opposite side of the highway. And that time had been at night. This was much brighter...The officer at the police tape line ushered her to Abe and then went back to his post.

"Thanks for coming," Abe said, his expression grim. "She's right this way."

He led her to a tarp that covered the body close to the pier. It was still on hard packed sand and while footprints were everywhere, Henrietta expected it was difficult to find a set that might belong to the killer. Or was it so much the killer or the one who deposited the body there? That would be hard to know.

"I know this won't be easy," Abe said, looking up at her from where he squatted next to the tarp's edge, "but just a quick look, all right?"

Henrietta nodded, taking a shallow breath as he pulled back the tarp. The dark hair of the woman looked the same as she'd seen in the house. While she didn't want to look any further, she looked over the woman's features.

"That's her," she said, turning away and putting a hand to her mouth. She stepped away, taking deep breaths of the sea salt air as it came off the water.

"I'm sorry, Henrietta," Abe said. "I know that's not easy."

"No, but it's necessary."

"That is Anne McGill, by the way."

Henrietta nodded. She'd thought as much. "Does she have family?"

"No, we had to have a neighbor come by to identify her before you. I just wanted to make sure that this was the body you'd seen in the house."

"Do you believe that it was there then?"

He looked down at her with slight amusement. "We brought in a cadaver dog which alerted on the spot you'd pointed out in the kitchen. I believed you before that, but that was the evidence we needed. Then we got the call about this body this morning. The M.E. will have to tell us time of death though. That will help with the timeline of all of this."

She nodded. "Why was she moved, that's my main question."

"I don't know. It's not readily apparent what killed her either," he admitted, though she had a feeling he should have by the grimace that followed his words.

"No marks then?"

"Not that we can see."

Henrietta nodded. "Sad."

"Very."

They stood in silence, looking out at the water in the quietness of the early morning.

Finally, Abe turned to her, "Well, that's all we need. You are free to go."

She felt like he was going to say, 'For now' but withheld the words. Why that was the case and why she felt that way she couldn't be certain but it bothered her.

Clearly, at least from her perspective, she was not involved in this in any way, but was it possible she would have to prove that?

"Where were you last night?" he asked, before she could leave. His words echoed her thoughts and sent a shiver up her spine.

"At the shop, actually. Well, in my apartment above it. I worked from the afternoon until closing then stayed home. Why, if I may ask?"

"Just collecting all the details."

She wanted to laugh and point out to him that there was no way she could have hauled a body, even one of a woman who was as petite as Anne, to this location by herself. She was a strong woman but not *that* strong. Unless...

Was it possible that Abe thought she had a part in this and Ralph had helped her?

It was ridiculous, and yet she had to see it from his perspective as a detective. He had to cover all angles, no matter how ridiculous they may seem. He was responsible to no one other than the law.

"Goodbye, Abe," she said, resting a hand lightly on his forearm before turning to walk up the beach back to her car.

"Thanks again, Henrietta," he called after her.

When she got back to her apartment she made herself a quick cup of coffee before going down to relieve Olivia of her duties until the afternoon.

"I'm back, thank you for stepping in."

Olivia looked up from where she perched on the stool behind the computer. Her face was pale and she looked unwell.

"Oh dear, you should have said you weren't up to it. I would have kept the shop closed."

Olivia offered a tired smile. "It's all right. I feel like I've let you down this last week."

"Nonsense," she smiled and patted the woman's hand. Then a thought occurred to her.

"How long have you been ill?"

Olivia shrugged. "It started about a week ago. I'm going to the doctor tomorrow if it's not better by the end of today."

Then, in the bleakness of two murders and her friend being in jail, Henrietta felt something as close to joy as possible.

"Ah yes, maybe you *should* go to the doctor."

Olivia missed Henrietta's mischievous smile but nodded in response when she picked up her purse. "I'll try to be back for my afternoon shift as long as I'm better."

"No problem, Olivia. Just let me know."

She watched the woman leave allowing herself a moment of normalcy before she turned back to the day's work. There was much to be done, but she worked quickly and by the time Jacob came in mid-morning, she was at a good stopping place.

"I'm glad you're here," she said as the young man came in and dropped his backpack in the back room.

"Why's that?" he said with a grin.

"I received an email."

"Yeah?" His eyes brightened.

She brought it up on her account on the shop computer to show him and he seemed to read it through several times.

"I think he knew."

"What?" she asked, trying to understand what the young man was talking about.

"I think he knew that we were tracking the email you sent."

"Really?"

"Well, first of all, we sent your email to him on this account," he opened the shop's email. "But he replied to *your* personal email."

Henrietta blinked. "I hadn't even thought of that."

"I'm not sure how he would have known the original email was traceable since I'm pretty good at covering my tracks, but I think he figured it out. Do you think this email is from him?"

Henrietta's eyebrows rose. "You don't think it is?"

"I don't know, but I'll work on tracing it *if* you think it's him."

Henrietta considered the words on the screen. She'd barely had honest contact with her nephew and wasn't sure *how* to tell. Then a thought occurred. "My sister. I think she'd know."

"All right," Jacob said, looking hopeful. "You can show that to her and then let me know. I'll put in the work, it's not that, I just want to make sure…"

"That it's worth it. I completely understand." She smiled at him and then considered the best way to break the news to her sister that her son had replied to his aunt, not his mother.

"You want to what?" The noise in the background made it difficult for Henrietta to fully understand Ralph.

"I want to take a look at some of the properties in town that Mark was looking to buy or had bought for his clients."

Henrietta looked at her to-do list for the rest of the day. Since Olivia had phoned and said she was doing better, Henrietta knew she could be spared from the shop.

"All right. Where should I meet you?"

"Corner of North and Main?"

"I'll be there in," she checked her watch. "Ten minutes."

"Gotcha." Ralph hung up and Henrietta set about getting ready to go. It would only take her a few minutes to get to the location Ralph had said but she wanted to make sure she had a few key items with her.

Minutes later she was in the car and on the way to the meeting location. She found an easy parking space on the street and walked a block to find Ralph waiting for her on the exact corner.

He wore a baseball cap with a sports team logo she didn't recognize on it. Then again, Henrietta wasn't really into sports so it wasn't difficult to find a team she hadn't heard of.

"I wasn't expecting a call from you today," she admitted as she joined him.

"I was doing some digging last night and went back

to the angle we'd been thinking of about Mark's sudden interest in the business he was looking to buy. Scott also found something," he said, beckoning her to follow him.

"What's that?" Henrietta joined him as they crossed the street.

"He found that Mark was actually working for Anne as well."

"What?"

"That's what I said. It seemed that Anne was the backer behind the purchase of Sassy's shop."

Henrietta had called and told Ralph about what she'd found, and he'd promised to look into it, though she hadn't expected him to find anything quite like this.

"So, she wanted Sassy's shop? But why?"

"We don't know but Scott's guess was that it was *for* DWC."

"How so?"

They continued walking up the street and Ralph pointed to the building they'd go to first before he answered.

"Remember those payments into Anne's account? Scott did trace them to a lesser known arm of DWC. It looks like they were not only paying her a stipend, they had also given her purchasing power for them. Scott's still trying to decode her email—that's how you know it's more than what it looks like—but she might have been scouting out locations and then working with Mark to cover it all up?"

"But why," Henrietta said, shaking her head.

"My theory is that DWC doesn't have the best appeal around here. After everything that happened with Seamus," he grimaced and looked over at her, "I think people would start to raise some red flags if DWC was buying up a lot of land."

"I understand that, I mean, I wouldn't want to sell my shop to them, that's for certain," she shivered at the mere thought, "but what is so important about these buildings? Are they trying to buy the town?" Henrietta laughed at the thought.

"I don't know but here we are," he motioned to the building they were next to, the door covered by paper on the inside. He reached out and pulled it open.

"Did you arrange this with them?" she asked, shocked.

"Nope."

She followed Ralph inside, wishing he would have better explained himself, but instead she came in to find a man in his mid-to-late forties pulling down strips of wallpaper.

"Hey ya, Joe."

The man turned a grinning face back at Ralph. "Hey, buddy," he said walking toward them, "good to see you."

Ralph nodded. "You too. This is Henrietta."

"Name's Joe. Nice to meet you," the man said, shaking her hand.

"You too," she said, looking to Ralph for more of an explanation.

"Joe here works for the previous owner. He's taking down some things in accordance with the new owner."

"Ah," Henrietta said, now understanding who she was dealing with.

"He's gonna let us poke around here and the building next door."

"They were both sold?" Henrietta said.

"Yep," Joe said, shaking his head. "It's a shame too."

"Why is that?" she asked.

"I've known both owners for a long time. Next door was a pet store and this was a travel agency."

"I remember," Henrietta said, trying to think back to when she'd seen them go out of business.

"And there was no reason to sell, I mean they were both doing well from what I understood."

"Really?" Usually people didn't up and sell profitable businesses.

"Yep, it's why I agreed when Ralph said he wanted to poke around. I mean, something's fishy with all of this—and I'm not just talking about the fish tanks left next door."

"What do you think isn't right, Mr.—uh, Joe?" Henrietta had found that oftentimes people's intuition was better than actual fact. Not always, but occasionally.

"I can't rightly tell you, but I got the feeling from

Mr. Mercer—that was the pet store owner—that he was forced into selling."

"That right?" Ralph said, eyeing Henrietta.

"Yep. I mean, he doesn't really take me into his confidence, mind you, but he did seem to hint at the fact he wasn't happy he was selling."

"What about the owner of this place?"

"That's an even stranger story," Joe said, shaking his head. "I asked him point blank—I've known the guy since high school and all—and he said he *had* to sell. There was no way around it. I asked him if it was money related or something, but he said it was nothing like that. But he got real green when I pushed him so I stopped."

"Interesting," Henrietta said, her brow furrowing as she took in the bare space. "And the new owners asked you to take care of these things?"

"Not exactly. It was what the old owners agreed to in their sales statement. To leave the space a certain way."

"Which is?"

"Empty."

"And wallpaper counts for that? Seems a bit much, don't you think?"

"This was more from the past owner, he made a stink about making sure it was *clean*. I think he was afraid he was going to get sued or something for leaving wallpaper behind. I guess the less you leave to the new owners the better. Still, seems excessive. This was just done a few months back anyway."

"It looked like it was a nice addition," Henrietta mused.

"That's what I thought." Joe shrugged. "Either way, go ahead and look around. I'll just be doing this."

"Have you met the new owners?" Henrietta asked.

"Nope. Don't suppose I will either. I know they went through that Mark what's-his-name guy. Never really liked him in high school, but excuse me—shouldn't talk ill of the dead."

Henrietta shrugged and Ralph thanked the man as they began to look around the office.

"What do you think made profitable business owners sell their property?" Henrietta asked when they'd moved from the front room into one of the back offices.

"I don't know, but it sounds like some stiff coercion."

"Sounds similar to what Sassy was facing. I mean, her business could have been ruined by the fake documentation and by the time everything was straightened out, she wouldn't be able to pay on her loan."

"She'd be forced to sell."

"Exactly." Henrietta nodded.

"You think that these owners were also forced into selling?"

"Yes, I do." She looked around the office but there

was nothing remarkable about it. "Though I don't understand why. I mean, it's a nice building but…what is the end goal?"

"Not sure we're going to get to know that."

She shrugged. "You know what we could do though," she looked over at her friend. "We can take a closer look at these buildings."

"Why don't you go to the County Clerk's Office and take a look at the blueprints and I'll see if I can't get in touch with the fella who owned this place before. I'll see if I can convince him to tell me what Mark had on him."

"Good idea. If we could prove there were others out there also being blackmailed into selling perhaps that would take some of the focus off of Sassy."

Ralph nodded and Henrietta left the building with a farewell wave to Joe. She made her way across the street, thankful the courthouse wasn't far away, and prayed that the blueprints would be public record. She was going to find a connection if it was the last thing she did.

## 12

SEVERAL HOURS later Henrietta had a large stack of copies from the County Clerk's office, and was on her way to meet Ralph at Gina's coffee shop. She pulled into her parking space in front of the shop and hustled into Espresso Yourself.

"Got you a vanilla latte," Ralph said, indicating a spot for her.

"Thanks." She slid onto the chair and deposited the papers in front of Ralph. "Basements."

"Huh?" he said, noisily sipping his mocha.

"They all have basements with reportedly connected tunnels."

"Tunnels? What are you talking about?"

Henrietta took a moment to sip her latte, enjoying the extra sweetness of the vanilla before she spread some of the papers out.

"The highlighted portions are what I'm talking

about. I stared at these schematics for what felt like days, but nothing seemed special about them until I lined them up on a large table—bless Mable for letting me use their conference room." Henrietta pointed to the bright yellow marked sections. "These are all the basements and see," she shuffled some papers around.

"They connect?"

"It looks that way."

Ralph leaned forward, studying the papers. "This is really something," he admitted. "You think that's why DWC wants them? But why? What good will basements—connecting or otherwise—do for them?"

Henrietta frowned. "That is the one thing I couldn't figure out."

"Oh, just that?" He made a face and she laughed.

"It got me thinking about those tunnels in Port Angeles. You remember that case?"

"Of course I do, but what does that have to do with these tunnels?"

"I don't know exactly. I wondered if maybe they were interested in setting up some type of tourist thing like they have in Port Angeles."

"Seems a little too altruistic."

"That's what I thought but maybe they want to bring in people? I mean, what else will they do with empty buildings."

"I haven't the faintest."

"What did you find out?" she said, still staring at the documents in front of them.

Ralph whistled. "It's a doozy."

"What is?" she asked, looking up.

"I met with Travis Ricardo, the owner of the travel agency, and he had a lot to say after I convinced him I was looking into the reason why he sold his business."

"What did he say?"

"He finally admitted that he *was* being blackmailed—"

"As we thought—"

"Yes," Ralph shot her a look for interrupting. "He was having an affair with the pet shop owner's wife."

Henrietta's eyes went wide. "Uh oh.'"

"You got that right. It's an ugly web, for sure. I think the woman must have had a hand in convincing her husband to sell when Mark came calling since she already knew there was leverage."

"That is just terrible," Henrietta said, shaking her head.

"Sounds like DWC will stop at nothing to get what they want."

"But would they stop at murder?" Henrietta looked over at Ralph to see what he thought.

"If they thought they could get away with it, maybe."

"So how does Anne figure in to all of this? If the note she left on my windshield was forged, or part of it, then who was it originally intended for?"

"She was working with—for?—Mark who was working with—for?—DWC. Somewhere in there is the problem."

Henrietta sat up straighter. "What if the note was meant for Mark?"

"So, Anne was telling Mark to stay away from her or she'd tell the police what he'd done."

"Which would be the blackmail."

"And perhaps when she found out that she wasn't just purchasing real estate on the up and up she wasn't okay with it."

"So," Henrietta surmised, "DWC—or Mark for all we know—killed her."

"But then Mark was killed."

Henrietta tilted her head to the side. "Cleanup?"

Ralph frowned. "Maybe. But it also accomplished a goal for them."

"Sassy in jail and her establishment discredited if she's convicted."

"Yet another business to add to their arsenal."

Henrietta shivered and sipped her coffee again. "This is dirty business, Ralph. If DWC is behind it, which will be difficult, if not impossible, to prove I'm sure, then we have to figure out what they are up to. I—"

Just then the door opened, and Henrietta looked up to see Detective Paige walking toward her. She didn't like the look on his face.

"Hello Abe," she said in a cheery voice, trying to ignore the concerned look on his face.

"Hi Henrietta, Ralph," he dipped his head to them both then huffed out a breath. "I hate to do this,

Henrietta, but I need to take you down to the station for questioning."

Her eyebrows rose and Ralph immediately protested. "See here, kid, you can't just take—"

"It's all right, Ralph," she said, resting her hand on his arm. "What, may I ask, do you want to talk about?"

"The death of Anne McGill."

"You've got to have marbles for brains if you think Henrietta had anything to do with it."

"I don't think she did," Abe admitted, "but I can't be seen having bias toward anyone. I'd be lax if I didn't explore every avenue."

Henrietta stood, finishing off her latte and tossing the cup in the trash near their table. "Then let's go."

"Henrietta—"

"It's all right, Ralph." She smiled up at Abe. "We're just going to have a chat. Take care of these papers for me and see if Scott has anything up his sleeve."

He frowned but then reached down to pull the papers together, glaring as she turned to go back to the police station with Abe. She hoped that Ralph had heard her double meaning in talking with Scott, but it was entirely possible that Ralph was too upset with Abe to take notice. Either way, she knew she had nothing to fear if she told the truth.

Henrietta stared into Abe's eyes after the question he'd asked. She could hardly believe it, but she wanted to think that he'd asked her due to some type of professional duty.

"Did you really just ask me if *I* killed Anne McGill?"

"I did." His features remained unmovable.

"Oh Abe," she sighed, and crossed her legs under the metal table. "I did *not* kill that poor woman. The first time I even saw her was in her house, on the floor, already dead."

"I have a witness saying they saw you enter her residence the day of the tasting."

"A witness—" Henrietta couldn't hide her surprise. "I can assure you I've never been to that house before aside from the day I called the police." Then something occurred to her. "Your witness wouldn't have blonde hair and dress fashionably?"

By the faint twitch at the corner of Abe's right eye she could tell she'd hit the nail on the head.

"Because, if that is your witness, you'll find that she will not appear in court. In fact, the name she gave you is likely a fake and you won't find her at the address she provided."

He narrowed his eyes and then looked to the two-way mirror behind her, giving a small nod. He was likely sending someone to go check on her assertions. To Henrietta it was obvious, Anita Black was making trouble for her even though she knew that it wouldn't truly put Henrietta in jail. What was the woman's plan? To tie her up at the police station then?

"Can you tell me what you know of Mark Wharton?"

Henrietta accepted his change of subject and filled him in on what she'd learned about the man so far. She even included a few guesses she had about his true employer, but short of being labeled a conspiracy theorist, she didn't mention the Deep Water Corporation. She wouldn't do that until she had absolute proof.

"So you knew that he was going to blackmail Sassy?"

"I only learned this the other day. I confronted Sassy about it and she admitted to it. She didn't share it because, well," she shrugged, "it sounds incriminating."

"It does," he admitted.

"But she's not the only one who faced blackmail to sell."

"Go on," he said.

She shared what she and Ralph had found that day. "Though I'd caution you it's not my news to tell, exactly."

Abe nodded. "We can look in to that."

A knock sounded on the door and frowning, Abe stood. "Be right back."

She watched him go and stared down at her hands. It was disconcerting, to say the least, to be held in a room like this while not working with the police but feeling as if they were working against you.

Then she thought of her sister and Calvin and Jacob. She still hadn't heard from the young man and she'd been so caught up with Sassy's case that she hadn't talked to her sister in a few days. Was Clementine worried? Was she not calling due to what Henrietta had called her out on before?

Suddenly the thought that her sister wasn't coming to her and sharing her true feelings worried Henrietta more than not having any news to share with her. She reached for her phone only to remember that it was held at Abe's desk. She felt a little like a criminal and she didn't like it.

"Anita," Henrietta said, her voice low.

She would pay that woman back for her meddling, lies, and unscrupulous dealings with the DWC.

"Well," Abe said, bursting into the room. She caught sight of Ralph standing in the hallway with Scott next to him. So, he had gotten her hidden message after all.

"It turns out that you have very good, very detailed friends, Henrietta."

She smiled back at Abe. "They are your friends too."

"Thankfully. Though I have a feeling all bets would be off with Ralph if I'd arrested you."

"You weren't going to do that."

He met her gaze and finally cracked a grin. "I wasn't."

"What did they show you?" she asked, curious as to what Scott had found in such a short amount of time.

"It appears that, in a slightly illegal move, Scott found out the time of Anne's death and, seeing as how Sassy was in jail already and you were taken in to custody, he came up with your whereabouts the day and time in question."

"Did he now?"

Abe smirked. "There you are in H.H. Antiques window putting up decorations, plain as day and time stamped by the camera across the street," he sighed.

"I'll have to thank Mr. Dutton for his security camera placement."

Now Abe just rolled his eyes. "But one more thing before you go," he said.

"Yes?"

"You know more than you're sharing. Does it involve Sassy or her case?"

Henrietta thought about how to answer that. "I do, and I don't." She held up a hand. "And before you charge me with being an obstruction," she winked, "it's not that I'm unwilling to share it's that I don't have true evidence. It's a lot of conjecture and the beginning stages of the full picture."

He leaned back, assessing her.

"All right. I'll accept that with the caveat that you'll tell me when you *do* have the full picture?"

"Why, Detective Paige, when have I ever tried to take the law into my own hands?"

His only reply was a laugh.

---

"HENRIETTA, please tell me you were not about to get arrested."

Henrietta looked up from the box of trinkets she'd picked up off the back room table. "I was not about to get arrested."

Olivia's eyes narrowed. "Scott called to say he'd be late to our lunch because he was looking up security footage of you."

"Sorry about making him late," she said with a smile.

"That's not the point," Olivia put a fisted hand on her hip. "Why was he needing to do that in the first place?"

"Because your husband is a master of computer surveillance."

"Henrietta," Olivia's tone left no room for argument and Henrietta smiled.

"Don't worry dear, I'm fairly certain Abe wouldn't have had enough evidence to hold me. I think Anita Black fed him a fake report about seeing me just to...I don't know, tie me up? Irritate me? That woman *is* getting on my nerves."

"Henrietta..." Olivia was at a loss for words.

"It's all right," she said, patting Olivia gently on the

cheek. "Things are going just the way they should, now."

It was clear Olivia didn't know what that meant and Henrietta wasn't sure she could explain it yet either. They had a clear motivation for Anne's murder—if the note she'd found was intended for Mark—and if Mark had gotten too greedy or in the way for DWC then his murder was explained. The biggest question now was the reason for DWC to be purchasing all of the buildings they could in town and how they'd come up with the blackmail on each owner.

Just then the front door opened and Jacob rushed inside. He had what Henrietta might have categorized as a 'wild look' in his eyes and, sensing he had something to share with her about her nephew, she moved to meet the young man.

"What is it Jacob?"

He took a deep breath, calming his breathing as if he'd run to the shop from his car. "I found him."

Henrietta blinked. "Found…Calvin?"

He nodded, glancing over her shoulder where Olivia had gone back to what she'd been doing before. "Do you want me to tell you here or…?"

Henrietta thought for a moment. "Let's go upstairs." Then, turning to Olivia she said, "We'll be down in a few minutes."

As a testament to her character, Olivia didn't question Henrietta's actions. It felt wrong, keeping her friend out of the loop, in a way, but it was personal business, not part of the case she knew about.

They walked up the stairs, Sepia racing up in front of them. The cat always seemed to know when Henrietta was going to their apartment, no matter where she'd been sleeping before that. She was likely looking for the food bowl that would have some remnants of dried cat food in it and because she was feeling hopeful, Henrietta would add a little extra for the feline.

"Please, have a seat," she said, gesturing to the sitting area that was right off the kitchen. "Just going to feed the cat a little."

Jacob eased down onto the sofa and Henrietta placed a small cup of dried food in the bowl. The cat immediately went to work on it. "Enjoy that," she muttered to the cat who seemed to be doing that very thing.

"Well," Henrietta said, choosing an armchair across from the young man, "What have you found?"

Jacob shook his head. "He is very good at covering his tracks, or he hired someone who was, but I was finally able to get the IP address of the location of the email he sent to your private email. Somehow he had to have known we'd traced the other one—though I don't know how he could have found that out."

Jacob seemed to slip into problem solving mode and Henrietta said, "And, where is he?"

"Right. Sorry," Jacob ran a hand through his hair. "You won't believe it. He's in Seattle."

Henrietta blinked rapidly. "So close?"

"Yeah. Crazy, right?" Jacob leaned forward, warming to his subject. "And, since I was able to find out where he is—some cheap motel on the south side of town—I traced that back through the system. I think he's going by the name Ted Henry. I found a train ticket, a few rental cars, and a bus pass made out to that name that makes a kind of odd line across the country to the West coast."

"He must have documents that state that's his name then, huh?" she said.

"Yes. I'm fairly certain it's him though."

"And why is that?" She wasn't skeptical exactly, but she didn't want to negate the fact that this Ted person could be impersonating her nephew. That had happened to her before.

"I can understand your hesitation," Jacob admitted, "but I'm pretty sure it's him. Ted Henry didn't exist until two days before Ralph landed in Virginia. He has the same personal information as your nephew, and your nephew seems to have dropped off the face of the earth. I'm still working on a visual connection, but I'm pretty sure it's him."

"And do you know why he's in Seattle? It seems like a bit of a coincidence for a man who apparently doesn't want any contact with his family."

"I'm not sure yet. Like I said, he's at a motel so it's

not a permanent residence, but I can't seem to find a connection."

She nodded slowly. "Jacob, I'm going to need you to get me an address. To where his motel is."

Jacob met her gaze but didn't speak for nearly a full minute. "Henrietta—" he finally began.

"Please," she said, holding up a hand, "he's my nephew."

She knew there were many arguments to combat that. He was actively hiding from his family. He had connections, though distant, to the Chicago mob. He wasn't seeking out a relationship with his family…And yet Henrietta knew she had to see him.

Still, the nagging question in her heart was whether or not she should tell her sister about this or wait until after she'd spoken with her nephew?

"I'll get you the address," Jacob said with a forced smile.

"Thank you," she said, leaning forward and smiling back at him. "You really are a great sleuth."

She could see her words pleased him, but she could also sense the hint of worry left behind on the boy's face. And wasn't there a hint of worry in her own heart for likely the same reasons?

## 13

HENRIETTA HADN'T PLANNED on going to Sassy's shop. When she'd left H.H. Antiques she'd merely needed to get out of the house. To think through the information Jacob had shared with her about Calvin, but also to gain perspective on Sassy and the murder of Mark and now Anne.

They were linked. Henrietta knew that much and she assumed Abe was coming to that conclusion as well, but *how*. That was the most pressing question. The Deep Water Corporation had something to do with it as well, but Henrietta couldn't begin to know what that would be.

She pulled all the information she had on the DWC to mind. Initially they had wanted to sponsor a boat race to Canada. It had looked like a corporation coming into town and supporting efforts to grow the town. It had *looked* good. But then it had been discovered that they were more interested in what they could smuggle out in those boats. Of course, DWC hadn't been directly linked to smuggling and yet...the idea was there.

They had also stepped up their involvement in town functions as a large sponsor and then one of their organizations had blackmailed the mayor. While Mayor Lawrence seemed to know nothing about their intention, there was a deeper reason, Henrietta was sure.

And now this—DWC buying up properties that were linked only by the presence of basements and the use of blackmail. Again, she was positive no direct link to DWC would be found, they covered their tracks too well for that, but she had a feeling there had to be something—some connection they'd overlooked.

Now, as her mind cycled through questions and possibilities she looked up to find she was at Sassy's shop, the front window boasting a 'Closed' sign which made Henrietta sad. She knew her friend had been blackmailed by Mark but now Mark was dead. Perhaps he had gotten greedy and wanted more than his fair share of the sale. Was that why he'd been killed? And why Anne?

More importantly, *who* had killed them?

"Interesting to find you here, Henrietta."

The voice, like ice crystals shattering, drew Henrietta around. "Anita Black. The Deep Water

Corporation's henchman." She added the last part and felt petty, but what was done was done.

Anita laughed. "Hardly. What, may I ask, are you doing in front of my property?"

"Your...what are you talking about?'

"I may be a little premature, but trust me—this lovely little shop is coming under new management soon."

"Let me guess. The DWC's ownership?"

Anita merely smiled.

"Well, until there is hard evidence to that fact, you have no claim on this shop, but my dear friend Sassy does."

Anita's eyes narrowed. "You so freely associate with murderers?"

"I freely associate with those who are wrongly accused." Henrietta held the woman's gaze. "Did you know Anne McGill?"

Anita frowned in thought. "The woman whose body was found on the beach? No, I can't say I did know Anne."

"Odd, seeing you there near her house and then hearing that you have an interest in these buy-ups. Seems you would have crossed paths with a fellow DWC employee."

"I can assure you, there are no ties between Anne and DWC. Directly."

The way Anita added *directly* made Henrietta

certain that they wouldn't find any ties. Yet another dead end.

"Good day," Henrietta said, turning on her heel.

"Henrietta," Anita called after her, "this town will be reborn. You'll see. And it will all be because of DWC."

Henrietta didn't deign to respond but it did make her wonder, yet again, what DWC's interest in Heart's Grove could possibly be. They were a small, tight-knit community. They had a strategic placement that kept them close to the Olympic National Forest as it did Seattle and Canada. There were natural resources and a rich history, but other than that Heart's Grove was nothing more than a hometown community.

Wasn't it?

But it was clear that Anita and the DWC had something else in mind. Something big and, likely, something bad planned. Henrietta just needed to find it out and stop it.

Her phone rang as she walked at a brisk pace away from where she'd left Anita drooling at the door of Sassy's shop.

"Yes?" she answered, not even bothering to look at caller ID.

"Hey Henrietta, this is Scott." She slowed to catch her breath.

"Hi Scott, what is it?"

"I've got some further information on the other attendees at the tasting. Thought you might be interested in knowing what I found."

She looked down the next few blocks and could just make out the Gershwin Private Investigators' office sign. "I'll be there in...five minutes."

"Oh," he sounded surprised, "Okay. See you then."

She hung up and kept up her fast pace. Perhaps this was the break they needed to clear Sassy's name.

---

"And you were just looking into them...why?" Henrietta asked.

Scott shrugged. "You know. No stone left unturned."

"But I don't understand. I thought Abe would have been all over the others at the tasting."

"Oh, he was," Scott assured her. "I have found that he is very thorough, but there are some things he... can't see?"

"You speaking nonsense, boy?" Ralph said, coming from down the hall and setting his mug in the small sink at the back of the office.

Scott made a face. "Good morning to you too, Mr. Grouchy."

"I just want this case solved," Ralph admitted, leaning up against the partition that separated each desk area of the front room. "What did you find?" he said, sounding more congenial than before.

"Well, as I was saying," Scott shot his father a look, "I think that Abe looked into this couple and thought things were fine, but he didn't look far enough back."

"Seems odd," Henrietta said, "He's very thorough."

"He is, but they did a really good job of creating this new life for themselves."

"Just to be clear," Ralph said, "We're talking about the newlyweds?"

"Yes. Angela Lambert and Tim Watt. Or, now, Angela and Tim Watt."

"And what's their crime?"

"This isn't Angela's first marriage. In fact, Lambert is her maiden name but she was Angela Young before marrying Tim. When you look into her history, she was married to Tim's former best friend —Carson. Together, they were sold a house by—you guessed it, Mark Wharton—that had structural issues."

"Oh no," Henrietta said.

"Oh yes. At the time that this happened it was actually Mark's side business—Crown Housing LLC— that was listed on the sale and documents. Then, a few years after the sale, there was a storm and—"

"Oh my."

"Oh my is right. Angela's husband, and Tim's best friend, was killed. Angela was away on a business trip and came home to find Carson had been killed."

Henrietta thought back. "I think I saw the article about that. Such a tragedy."

"It wasn't immediately clear what had caused the

house to collapse and some pointed to the tree that had fallen, things like that," Scott said.

"What changed then?" Henrietta asked.

"That's the rub." He clicked a few keys. "It looks like Angela and Tim were working on purchasing a house and from speaking with their new realtor, they were talked into a home inspection. Angela was confused, said she'd never gone through that process before, and the realtor she was working with cited a few cases where homes had been poorly inspected and problems came along with that."

"It got her thinking," Ralph said, tracking along with the story.

"Yes. We can't know for sure, but I spoke with a lawyer—John Wright—who, while not disclosing everything, mentioned that Angela and Tim were planning on entering into a lawsuit with Mark."

"And then he showed up dead," Ralph said.

"When speaking with Mr. Wright did you find that they thought it would be a useful case?"

"How'd you know, Henrietta?" Scott asked.

She'd had a hunch but wanted to see what he said.

With her silence Scott continued. "John told me and told them that the likelihood that Mark would be charged with anything from so long ago—and with the house torn down now—was not likely."

"So, they took things into their own hands," Ralph mused.

"We can't confirm that," Scott pointed out.

"No, but we can look into it," Henrietta said. "Seems there was no end to the amount of people who wanted to kill Mark Wharton."

"Sassy was being blackmailed, the DWC wasn't happy—"

"Wait," Henrietta said, looking up at Ralph. "How do we know they weren't happy with him?"

"He's dead, isn't he?"

"Yes, and I assume that's good for DWC, just as Anne's death is good for them because if she'd gone to the police about Mark the DWC could have been implicated. But, how do we know that DWC was behind all of this?"

"We don't," Scott said.

"Exactly," Henrietta said, sounding defeated. "But maybe that's not the point right now."

"Come again?" Ralph said.

"I am fairly certain that, even if it comes out that Angela and Tim had something to do with Mark's death, and it was motivated by revenge, there was a motivating factor behind it."

"You mean DWC," Scott said.

"Yes." She nodded, pacing in front of Scott's desk. "It will be impossible to connect, I'm sure. She covers her tracks, but when the end result is DWC getting the buildings they want, they likely don't care who does their dirty work."

"She?" Scott said.

Henrietta looked up and met his gaze. "Anita Black.

I'm fairly certain she was behind all of this, but we need to get this information to Abe. Immediately."

Scott nodded. "I'll send it over right now."

Henrietta sighed and headed toward the door but Ralph stopped her before leaving.

"Hey, we'll get them."

She turned doubtful eyes toward him. "We don't know what they want of Heart's Grove and we don't know who they even are, except for their mouthpiece, Anita Black. And even she seems to be above the law."

"No one is above the law, you know that."

"I know, it just feels that way."

Gently, with slow, deliberate motions, Ralph reached up and cupped her cheek. "We'll get 'em. I promise."

Henrietta allowed his warm, calloused hand ground her in reality. She wasn't alone and, while they seemed to be up against a faceless entity with reach beyond their understanding, she trusted Ralph and their partnership.

"We will," she agreed.

## 14

HENRIETTA SAT in the front seat of Abe's detective car, the heater warming her feet. The man himself sat beside her as they looked out the large front window at the small, cape cod style home sitting on a bluff overlooking the ocean.

Then, as if in slow motion or like something you would see on a television show, officers came out with both Angela and Tim Watt in handcuffs between them. Angela's head bent low, hair covering her face, and Tim's expression was drawn.

"We still don't know who killed Anne," Abe said, his voice filling the once silent space.

"I think it was Mark."

She felt Abe's eyes on her. "Can you prove it?"

"Not yet."

He chuckled. "If you let me in to what you're

thinking maybe I could help. We do, eventually, catch killers," he said, pointing toward the couple being ushered into the police car.

"I know you do. And it's not that I don't have confidence in you. It's that I don't have enough to go on yet. Hunches don't sign warrants," she said. It sounded like a phrase she'd heard on a television show.

"Henrietta," Abe said, turning toward her in the seat. "I know Scott came on to this couple in researching who else was at the tasting, but did you know?"

She turned to meet his gaze. "No. I had no idea." She wasn't going to tell him she'd thought that the DWC had a hand in it, or that she *still* thought they did.

"I was convinced it was Sassy. I was building my case. I thought you'd even handed it to me when we found out she was being blackmailed."

"I know," she said. "If I hadn't known Sassy as I do, I might have thought the same."

"But you believed in her innocence."

"Always."

The car, containing the couple whose purchase history had included the chilies used in Mark's murder, was now pulling away from the curb.

"Shall we head back to the station so you can see your friend?"

Henrietta smiled. "Yes, please."

They drove in silence, Henrietta lost in thought.

When they reached the station and went inside she was surprised to see a man—clearly a lawyer—standing with Angela and Tim.

"You go ahead," the lawyer was saying. "I'll be coming in to speak with you soon. Please refrain from answering any questions until I'm with you."

They nodded and were taken away and Abe moved forward to shake hands with the man. "Wright, good to see you."

"You too, Abe. Just bad circumstances."

"Sure is," Abe admitted. "Oh, this is Henrietta Hewitt, owns H.H. Antiques in town. Henrietta, this is John Wright. He's a lawyer but I don't hold that against him." The men shared a laugh.

"Nice to meet you, Mr. Wright." She looked between them. "How do you two know one another?"

Abe grinned. "Outside of work, I do have extracurricular actives, Henrietta. John and I met at the boat club. We sometimes sail together."

Henrietta nodded. "How lovely. Do you have your own practice, Mr. Wright?" She asked, smiling up at him sweetly.

"No, actually," he said with a kind smile. "I work for The Deep Water Corporation."

Henrietta's stomach clenched with this realization. What was a lawyer for the DWC doing working with the Watt couple? Was DWC paying the bill? This was yet another connection of DWC to these murders.

Before she could ask any more questions a petite

officer with dark brown hair popped her head into the reception area. "Uh, Mr. Wright? They're ready for you in room B."

"Thank you," he said with a nod to the woman. "And nice to meet you Miss Hewitt. Abe, see you around."

Henrietta merely nodded, watching the man go. This was growing deeper than she'd imagined but she had no hard evidence.

"Henrietta, it looks like you've seen a ghost."

She forced a smile. "Sorry, just anxious to see Sassy."

"Be right back," he said.

Then, only a few minutes later the doors opened and Sassy came out, carrying a paper bag of her affects and wearing the same outfit she'd come to the station in.

"Henrietta," she said, dropping the bag and embracing her friend. "I'm so happy to see you."

"Welcome back," Henrietta said with a smile. "Want to go home?"

Sassy nodded. "More than anything."

Henrietta bid farewell to Abe and they left out the front door. Once in the car, Henrietta turned to her friend.

"I need to stop by my shop before taking you home, if you don't mind?"

Sassy shrugged. "I don't care where we go as long as it's far, far away from the police station."

Henrietta had hoped she'd say that and took off to

the shop. When they arrived, she parked and turned to her friend.

"Why don't you come in really quick? I won't be long, but you don't want to be stuck in the car."

Sassy agreed and they took the front steps toward the shop which hosted a 'Closed' sign for the day. Sassy didn't seem to notice it.

When Henrietta stepped back to let her friend in the front door, she hid her smile and quickly closed the door behind her. "Right this way, to the counter section for a moment."

Again, Sassy merely followed directions until she stepped through the doorway and a shout rang out. "Welcome back!"

Friends lined the small, open area in front of the antique shop's desk. They were all smiling and clapping and a large banner that read, "Welcome Out Sassy" hung opposite the doorway.

"Oh my goodness," Sassy said, covering her mouth with tears falling down her cheeks. Some of her neighbors, shop supporters, and friends were there along with Gina, Ralph, Scott, Olivia and Jacob.

"I know it's not great timing, but I thought you needed a little happiness to welcome you back out into the real world."

Sassy's tears fell even more heavily, but she hugged Henrietta and turned to greet her friends.

"Great job on the surprise," Olivia said, coming up next to Henrietta. "You throw great parties."

"Keep that in mind," Henrietta said, smiling as she looked over at Olivia, "for when you want to announce your big news."

Olivia's eyes went wide and she looked over at Scott. "He told you, didn't he!" She shook her head.

"Hardly," Henrietta said, patting Olivia's arm. "My dear, I'm not a detective for no reason."

Olivia's responding laugh filled Henrietta's heart. "Yes, we're expecting, but I'd like to keep it a secret for now. Too many of my friends lost their first and I just…I can't bear it if that happens and so many knew."

"I understand, dear," Henrietta said, wrapping her arm around her employee and friend. "And you just let me know what time off you need if you're feeling unwell."

"You're the best, Henrietta," Olivia said.

Just then Ralph made his way toward them, eyeing the hug with suspicion. "What's going on?'

"Nothing," Olivia said, wiping a tear from her eyes, "I am just thankful for Henrietta in my life."

Ralph grunted and gave a quick nod, "I can get behind that."

Olivia left to join Scott where Sassy was regaling a small group with stories from 'the clink' as she put it, and Henrietta turned to look up at her friend.

"This case isn't done," she admitted.

"Not by a long shot," he agreed.

"But they arrested the guilty parties—I suppose that should make me happy."

147

Ralph looked down at her, his head turning to the side. "It's going to be okay, Henrietta. You and I both know that. DWC won't get away with whatever it is they're doing. We're smart. Abe's...smart," he said reluctantly which made her smile, "and we'll get to the bottom of this. Let's just celebrate Sassy being free. Let's celebrate the win."

She knew he was right and had a good point, and she wanted to celebrate. But she also couldn't help but think about what she had to do later that day.

"I'm going somewhere...this afternoon," she said, looking up at him.

"All right. Do you need me to come with you?" he asked.

"No," she'd thought about this and decided this was a trip for her and her alone to make. She'd called Clementine but she'd withheld the information about Calvin's location. Whether it may come back to bite her or not, she felt going alone was the right decision. "I've got to take a trip to Seattle."

"All right," he said.

She waited, expecting him to try and stop her or demand he go with her, but instead, he reached for her hand and held it. "I'll be here when you get back."

And in that freedom, in that release, she felt that she'd made the right choice. No matter what would happen when she met with Calvin, she would come back with more answers than she had before. And that, as Ralph would say, would be worth celebrating.

Check out the next adventure, *A Fatal Affair,* today.

Thanks for reading *Death by Dessert*. I hope you enjoyed the story. If you could take a minute and leave a review for me, that would be really appreciated.

The next story in the series is called *A Fatal Affair*. You can buy it now on Amazon.

If you would like to know about future cozy mysteries by me and the other authors at Fairfield Publishing, make sure to sign up for our Cozy Mystery Newsletter. We will send you our FREE Cozy Mystery Starter Library just for signing up. All the details are on the next page.

## FAIRFIELD COZY MYSTERY NEWSLETTER

Make sure you sign up for the Fairfield Cozy Mystery Newsletter so you can keep up with our latest releases. When you sign up, **we will send you our FREE Cozy Mystery Starter Library!**

**FairfieldPublishing.com/cozy-newsletter/**

Made in the USA
Columbia, SC
30 October 2024